THE SHOESHINE GUY

THE SHOESHINE GUY

JIM HEARN
AND
ED HEARN

Wisdom/Works
Published by Wisdom Works

jimhearn@jimhearn.com
ehearn@ec.rr.com
ehearn1234@gmail.com

Published 2019 – First Edition
Copyright © 2019 by Jim Hearn and Ed Hearn

ISBN 978-1-70652-744-2

Printed in the United States of America
Set in Adobe Garamond Pro
Editing and proofreading by Trent Armbruster and Tom Morris
Cover design and back cover photo by Sara Morris
Interior book design by Abigail Chiaramonte

*"A man's gift makes room for him
and brings him before great men."*

"Sometimes things happen in a person's life
that change him forever,
and
sometimes a person meets someone
who changes his life forever.

Both happened to me,
and
this story may do the same for you."

Jim Hearn

CHAPTER ONE

When I think back about the unusual circumstances that changed my life, I can hardly believe what really happened. I'll try to tell the story, detail by detail, so you can decide for yourself if you believe me. You'll have to form your own opinion. For me, the truth is stranger than fiction.

It all started one day as I was preparing to go to work, where I was a successful salesman at an upscale, used car dealership in Nashville, Tennessee.

I stood in my bathroom combing my hair, looking into the mirror, and thinking about the day ahead. All I could see was a handsome guy who had the world by the tail. My long-sleeved white shirt was heavily starched and complimented my fashionable suspenders, silk necktie, and cuffed black pants with razor sharp pleats. The outfit was topped off by my ascot cap.

As I walked out of the bathroom, a full-length mirror on

the living room wall assured me I was 'looking good.' Today was going to be a great day.

Glancing down, I noticed a light haze of dust on the top of my freshly polished wingtip shoes. All that was necessary to remove it was to slide the toes under the center cushion on my sofa to quickly wipe the dust away. I'd spent way too much effort polishing them the night before to leave for work with anything but perfection.

"Yep, that looks better," I heard myself say out loud to no one in particular.

Picking up a set of keys and my custom-engraved money clip from the entry hall table, I placed them in my right-front pocket and slipped my alligator wallet easily into my right-rear pocket. Just outside the front door of the apartment, positioned only forty feet away, was a beautiful demo car from the dealership that I'd left parked near the sidewalk. It was a bright and shiny, red 350-Z convertible, one of my rewards for being the top grossing salesman.

There's no question I make more money than all the other salesmen combined. The owner loves me, I thought. *I've made more money for him this year than he ever imagined.* That's what went through my mind as I started the car, put on my designer sunglasses, smiled and headed toward the interstate.

The 350-Z moved swiftly through traffic, passing the NFL football stadium just outside of downtown Nashville. After driving down the exit ramp, it wasn't long before I could see the familiar sign for the used car dealership of Buddy Victory Motors. Pulling in and rounding the first turn to the right, my pride soared as I parked in the reserved spot I'd earned by maximizing profits on every deal I'd finalized that month. A metal sign read, "Reserved for the salesman of the month." They could have just painted my name on it.

It was time again to cut a few deals, and I was ready for the challenge. Into the side door I went. I grabbed a quick cup of coffee and walked to the receptionist's desk.

"Good morning, Sue. How many calls have I had this morning?"

"No calls, yet. It's early, Gary. You do have a customer named Bill who's waiting to speak with you. He's in the front lobby and been there about ten minutes. I told him you'd be here shortly, if he was willing to wait."

Moving with a confident stride, I rounded the corner and entered our lobby to see Bill sitting and reading the morning newspaper. "Hey, Bill. How are you today? Are you here to talk about that beautiful Cobra Mustang you test drove yesterday?"

"Yeah. We need to talk about its total cost and the extras you'll include."

"No problem. Let's go into my office down the hall where we can have some privacy."

Once in the office, I took a seat behind the desk and motioned for Bill to take one of the other chairs and pull it to the front where we could talk. "Would you like a cup of coffee? I can ask Sue to get one for you."

"No. I'm fine."

"Well, here's the deal," I said. "We can include an extended warranty for an additional $3,000 over the $25,000 we originally talked about. That's $28,000 total, and the tax is included. I'd highly recommend you do that."

"Is an extended warranty that much?" Bill asked.

"Yeah, here's the thing. You'll get a tremendous benefit by having it, and it'll add a lot to the resale value of the car when it gets to be that time. You can't go wrong. All you have to do is bring a cashier's check for the total cost. You told me you didn't want to finance any of it. So…the question is, do you want it or not?"

"Yes I do," Bill replied. "I'll have the check for you later this afternoon."

"Good. When do you want to pick it up?"

"Today, if that's possible," he said.

"Let's do it at five o'clock this afternoon. We'll have it serviced, washed, and ready to go."

Bill stood and reached over my desk to shake my hand. He had a huge grin on his face. After the handshake, he turned and walked out of my office and quickly left through the front door of the dealership.

While adjusting my unique cap on my head, I thought, *Another one bites the dust! Today is definitely going to be a great day!*

Just as soon as Bill was out of my office, Joe Wilks, my sales manager, stepped in and closed the door. Joe was tall and stocky with an athletic build. His buzz haircut gave him a little of the military look.

In his right hand was a clipboard jammed full of paperwork. He stood looking at me, about to ask a question, but I first gave him a 'fist' gesture. "You don't have to ask," I said. "The answer is yes. I confirmed the deal with Bill."

I got up from my chair and did a little jig for Joe in

celebration. I couldn't help but start singing. "Another one bites the dust…Yeah. Another one bites the dust…Hey, Hey."

"Is the silver mustang the one you sold him?" Joe asked.

"Yeah. That's the one we just worked on the transmission. Hopefully, it'll hold up for a while. Fortunately for us, it'll soon be his problem to deal with.

"Is he coming in this evening to pick it up?"

"At five o'clock. That's the plan. I told him he needed to bring a cashier's check for $28,000."

"I thought he only needed $25,000?" Joe asked.

I replied, "He did." I couldn't keep the smile off my face. "But I told him we needed $28,000 and that would cover the warranty. That gives us an additional $3,000 in profit and more money in my pocket. You know that extended warranty costs us almost nothing. Pretty cool, huh? In the fine print on the warranty paperwork, we'll make sure it doesn't cover the transmission. I didn't tell him the extended warranty was included in the $25,000 from the start."

"I'll have to say, you're one sly fox. You make this dealership more money than all the other salesmen every month. Keep up the good work. By the way, how many deals have you closed so far this month?"

"If you'll check your records, I believe you'll find that cool mustang makes fifteen, and I've got another week to go in the month," I said.

"Fifteen? Awesome job! You're the MAN. Got anything else working at the moment?"

I looked down on my desk and quickly thumbed through a stack of notes and paperwork.

"Let's see. Johnson will probably take the Volvo. Matthews is a sure bet on the black Jeep. Turner loves that hot Lexus, and Baldwin can't do without the Mercedes convertible. Those should all be gone by Saturday. I'm on track to do over twenty cars this month."

Joe said, "Wow!" Then he stood at attention, clicked his heels, and saluted. "Carry on soldier...as you were."

CHAPTER TWO

After Joe walked out of my office, I leaned back in my chair, lifted my right foot, and placed it on the edge of my desk. There was a small scuff on the toe, so I took the shoe off and used a buffing cloth from my desk drawer to bring back the shine. I also buffed the other shoe and replaced the first one on my foot. *They both look much better*, I thought.

About that time, David Norton walked into my office and without hesitation took a seat in the chair in front of my desk. David was another salesman I'd worked with for a couple of years. Good salesman, but not as good as me. He was in his late forties, stocky build with dark brown hair.

"Hello, sir. I need a favor," David said.

"What?"

"I'd like you to shine my shoes."

Looking right into David's eyes, I said, "How long have we known each other?"

"About two years," David said.

"And how many times have I shined your shoes in that length of time?"

"Never."

"Exactly," I said. "And don't ask why, because you know why."

"Gary, I can't put that kind of shine on my shoes. It's impossible...and I was in the military. Why won't you do it for anybody else?"

"I shine my shoes to make me look good. If I shine your shoes, then you'll look as good as me. I do it to make me look good...not other people."

Joe Wilks entered my office and walked up to David's side. "David, Steve Barnes needs to see you in the finance office."

"You have to go now," I said. "We'll talk later. I'll bet if you worked on it, you'd be able to get a good shine on your own shoes."

Joe walked out with David right behind him.

I heard an announcement over the paging system. "Gary Neal. Come to Buddy Victory's office at your earliest convenience."

I thought to myself, *Surely...the big boss is calling his fearless leader of the pack to his office to praise him.*

On the way to Buddy's office, I passed two of the other salesmen in the hall, smiled and said, "Hello." Into Buddy's office I walked, through his open door, without even knocking. He was looking down at a piece of paper in deep concentration.

"What's up?" I asked.

"Have a seat."

I sat down in front of his desk in a chair that had been placed there for that purpose.

Before I had a chance to make a comment, Buddy said, "Well…you made the fast start bonus for the first half of the month…again." He extended his right hand. In it, he held a check. "Here you go. I guess you're going to take tomorrow off, since that's part of the bonus?"

"Absolutely," I said.

In response, Buddy made a face and let me know he wished I wouldn't.

"Don't use the guilt trip, captain. You know better." With a light chuckle and smile, I said, "Yeah, offer me a day off and then attempt to make me feel guilty for taking it. Good try."

I rose and started to leave Buddy's office with the nice bonus check. As I looked down at it in my hand, Buddy said, "Don't leave just yet. I want to talk with you about something important."

"What?"

"I know I've said this a dozen times already. I need you as a manager to teach the other salesmen your techniques."

"Buddy, we've had this conversation too many times in the past. What did I say the other times?"

"You said, NO. I thought that maybe you'd changed your mind and could see the benefits for yourself and the company by now."

"I appreciate the offer, Buddy, but I'm happy having the freedom to sell cars and earn the big commissions and bonuses."

"You and Joe Wilks would make a great team," Buddy said.

"I don't think I'd enjoy the team concept. My style is being a solo player. You know me. I'm sort of a Lone Ranger."

Buddy said, "Yeah, I know. I just don't totally understand why."

"Hey, if it ain't broke, don't try to fix it. Right?"

On my way out, Buddy stopped me by saying, "One more question."

"What?"

"You really get a kick out of yourself, don't you?"

I had to think about that one for only a few seconds. "Yes, I do!"

I then turned and left Buddy's office with a broad smile on my face. All that came to mind was a line from one of my favorite Frank Sinatra songs, *I Get a Kick Out of You.*

Back in my office, I checked myself out by using a full-view mirror hanging on the wall behind the door. I pitched my cap on top of the bookshelf, so I could see the whole package. *Looking good!* I thought.

After doing a little dance for my own amusement in front of the mirror, I sat down, and out of habit pulled a polishing cloth from my desk drawer. When I looked at my shoes, I realized they already had a high shine. The cloth was put away, and I just stared at them. As I was admiring the shoes, I'd swear I could see my reflection in the surface.

CHAPTER THREE

Two hours later, it was lunchtime. I didn't want to eat from the vending machine in the dealership waiting area after having experienced such a successful morning, so out the front door to my waiting 350-Z I went.

As I passed Sue at the front desk, I asked, "Is there anything I can pick up for you? I'm on my way over to the little diner a few miles away. You know the one. I want to get outside in the sunshine and enjoy the air moving through my hair in that beautiful convertible, as I zip down the interstate."

"Nope. Thanks for asking. I'm fine. Have a nice ride and lunch. I'll see you later."

Climbing into my smokin' demo, I couldn't imagine a better way to celebrate. In my wallet was a fat bonus check, the owner of the business was happy, and I was on top of the world. I lifted my sunglasses off the console, snapped on my seatbelt, and ran my fingers through my hair. As I turned on the radio, a very appropriate song was playing, *Summer Wind.*

Pulling away from the dealership, I noticed a smart-dressed, big man standing on the side of the road near the entrance ramp of the interstate. He was wearing a sporty hat, sunglasses, and a big smile just like mine. His thumb was in the air, and he looked to be friendly enough. The way my day had been going, I thought picking him up would be a nice thing to do.

I eased over to the side of the road, slowed to a stop, and asked, "Where are you going? Maybe I can give you a lift."

"Thanks for stopping. I'm just trying to get downtown. If you can take me with you for a few miles, it would be greatly appreciated."

"Hop in," I said.

"What a beautiful car! Thanks for picking me up."

There's no suitcase or any baggage, I thought, while looking at him. I found that unusual but didn't say anything.

Within a short distance, I entered the interstate and started to pick up speed. I leaned over so my new friend in the passenger seat could hear and said, "This little baby will fly when I give it the gas."

He just smiled and didn't make a comment.

About that time, my cell phone began to ring. I picked it up off the dash and accidently dropped it between my seat and the console. Starting to dig with my right hand, I realized I couldn't reach it.

There was no success on my first try. I just couldn't get my hand in far enough. Taking my eyes off the road briefly, I looked down to see exactly where the phone had ended up. The thought ran through my mind, *Come on, work with me.*

The man riding with me said, "Let me get it for you. You should be watching the road."

"No. I'll get it."

Just as that was said, I looked up, realized I was going way too fast, and noticed I was about to rear-end the car in front of me. Swerving to the right, I bumped the edge of an eighteen-wheel truck in the other lane. That knocked my car hard to the left. Before I knew it, we shot through the center, grass median and spun around. I was then hit on the driver's side by a vehicle which had been traveling in the opposite direction. My car flipped over and over several times. The crash occurred so quickly and was so forceful that I would have been thrown from the car, if I hadn't been wearing my seat belt. The horrendous impact instantly caused me to lose consciousness.

The next thing I was aware of, for only a moment, was a voice asking questions.

"Mr. Neal, are you with us? Mr. Neal, can you hear me? Mr. Neal, I need you to wake up. Come on, Mr. Neal, join us. Can you hear me? Can you say something? Do you know where you are? You've been in an accident and now you're in an ambulance on the way to a hospital."

"What's his blood pressure?" asked the first Emergency Medical Technician.

"75 over 35 and dropping quickly," said the second EMT.

"All right, we're on our way to the hospital. Can you say something, Mr. Neal? Say something if you can, OK?"

"How long has he been unconscious this last time?" asked the second technician.

"I'm not really sure."

"Are you assigned to him? I mean…is he one of yours?"

The first EMT looked at the other man and smiled slightly. "Yep."

"You're planning to take him down to the wire, aren't you?"

"Yeah, I've got to. This one is a real hard head. I have to take him as far as I can to get his attention."

With a concerned tone in his voice, the second EMT asked, "How much longer?"

Holding up his right hand, in an effort to stop additional questions, the first EMT said, "Hang on, we're just about there." At that moment, my body stiffened, and my head tilted back. A high-pitched beep was heard from the blood pressure machine. "OK. He's in defib. Get the paddles, but wait until I tell you to apply them."

After a full five minutes passed, the word was finally given to proceed. The second EMT put the paddles on my chest.

"Ready?"

"Yep. Go ahead."

The first technician administered a strong 'jolt' of electricity. Low-pitched, repetitious beeps were heard. "OK. We're good. Call the hospital and tell them what happened. Give them his numbers. Tell them we're only two blocks away."

Everything was fuzzy in my head. I think I came back to consciousness as a calm feeling moved through my body, so I just relaxed.

The first EMT leaned over and said directly into my ear, "Keep your eyes closed and listen to me. You're going to be OK. You're going to make it. Stay calm. This wreck happened for a reason. You're on your way to the hospital. They're not going to find anything wrong with you. From this moment forward, your life is going to change. Everything is not going to be just about you anymore. After you leave the hospital, it's going to take you a few days to get back to normal, but you will experience a 'new normal.' Listen very carefully. Once you get back to your regular schedule, I want you to start looking for the number 89. That number is important for you, to get a new direction in your life. Why this happened will be explained to you. Your new life will start immediately. Trust me, you're in good hands. If you understand what I've just said, squeeze my hand."

I must have squeezed his hand at that point because I remember hearing some additional comments.

"Good. Take care now. We're at the hospital, and they'll be taking care of you. You were in a very bad wreck. You have some blood on your forehead at the moment, and you'll be bruised up for a week or so. The good news is, you'll be fine, just as I told you a little while ago. This has all happened for a reason."

CHAPTER FOUR

Later, I found myself sitting on the edge of an examination table in the emergency room, elbows on my knees with my head in my hands. I was repeating what the voice in the ambulance had said to me.

"After you leave the hospital, start looking for the number 89. When you find that number, why this happened will be explained to you. Everything will be explained. 89...89... find 89."

About that time, a nurse walked in. "Are you OK? You were repeating 89...89...find 89, as I walked through the door."

"I'm not sure. My car...do you know what happened to it? There was another man riding with me when the accident occurred. I had just picked him up shortly before having the wreck. Was he hurt? I'd almost forgotten about him."

"The EMTs said your car was totally demolished. Just be glad you weren't. We have no record of anyone else being in the car with you. You must be imagining that. From what the EMTs said, you're lucky to be talking to me right now. Lucky too that no one else was hurt. The people in the car that crashed into you are all going to be fine. None of us can believe it. Do you want some water?"

"That would be nice. May I please make a quick call on your cell phone?"

She handed me her phone and said, "Sure, but make it fast. I'll be right back."

"I know there was someone else in the car with me," I said.

She pointed her finger at me as she began to leave. "There was no one else in the car. You must have imagined that. You stay right there. The doctor will be here soon."

Looking around the room, I couldn't believe what had taken place. It had all happened so quickly. Maybe I was just dreaming I'd had a passenger with me in the car. Thankfully, no one else had been hurt in the accident.

I dialed the number of my girlfriend, Abby. I was sure she would want to know about the accident, and that I was in the hospital not seriously injured.

"Hi, Hon. You're not gonna believe this. I'm at the hospital."

Abby asked, "Oh, my God. What happened?"

"I've been in a bad car accident. My demo is totaled, but I'm fine. I'm not really sure how that happened. It's all unreal."

"Are you hurt at all? Do you have anything broken?"

"Right now I'm still in the emergency room, in one of those little cubby holes waiting for the doctor, but I don't think they can find anything wrong with me. That's the really unusual part. Will you come and get me?"

"Which hospital are you in?"

"I'm at the same one your mother was in recently near West End Avenue."

"I'm on my way. I love you."

"Thanks, Hon. I need to go. The doctor just walked in. I love you, too. Bye."

Just as I was concluding the call, a doctor walked in holding a clipboard. "Hello, Mr. Neal," he said.

"Call me Gary."

"OK, Gary. How are you doing?"

At that moment, the nurse came back into the room with a cup of water and handed it to me. I gave her the cell phone. She turned around and started to leave the room.

As she neared the doorway, I said, "Thank you."

To the doctor, I said, "I was hoping you would be able to tell me how I'm doing."

"Well, I don't exactly know what to tell you. All I can truthfully say is that you're one lucky guy."

"What do you mean by that, doc?"

"Tell me what you remember…from the beginning."

"About what?"

"About everything…the entire wreck…everything," the doctor said.

The doctor then added, "There are a lot of things that just don't add up. Your vehicle flipped several times, and it was a convertible which offered no protection. People in that type of accident don't normally survive, much less have no injuries at all. You had some blood on your forehead when you came in. We're sure it was your blood but can't find the source. The only explanation we can come up with is that you were either cut or scratched and the wound has already healed. This whole thing is very strange…very strange indeed."

"I don't know anything about the blood."

As I took a drink of my water from the cup, my mind began to go back to the time of the accident.

"What I remember is that my cell phone rang. I dropped it between the seat and console of my car. While searching for it, I took my eyes off the road. Swerving to the right, I bumped into an eighteen-wheel truck. The next thing I can remember was the car spinning to the left, across the center median into the oncoming lane of traffic. The car then flipped over and over. Something hit me hard. I don't remember anything else until I was in the ambulance. I heard some beeps and felt something on my chest. I heard a voice telling me a bunch of stuff I tried to remember, and someone was holding my hand. After that, I woke up in the hospital."

"I'll say it again. You're one lucky guy."

"So, what's going on? Am I going to be OK?"

After a brief pause, the doctor said, "I hope so. But, you shouldn't be. I mean…you have no concussion…no fractures. Nothing is wrong. And, we have no confirmed answer for where the blood on your head came from. All the tests indicate everything is as it should be…like nothing happened. Actually, I would say you're a walking miracle. You should be dead. It's obvious someone was looking out for you. I would call this YOUR LUCKY DAY, if you believe in that sort of thing."

"What do you mean?"

The doctor pulled up a chair directly in front of me, sat down, and looked directly into my eyes. "When you were in the ambulance, you left us...for over five minutes, according to the two EMTs who were with you."

"What do you mean, I left?"

"I won't say you died, but something happened," the doctor said.

"What happened? Come on doc...just give it to me straight. Tell me what happened."

"I'm not sure. When you were in the ambulance, you started crashing. No heartbeat, no breathing, no blood pressure... nothing! The EMTs keep the exact time if you stop breathing or if they lose your vital signs. You completely left us for over five minutes. They had to use paddles. Then, all of a sudden, everything started back up again. Everything was back to normal. Your heart rate, breathing, and blood pressure were all normal. You were fine. You were still unconscious, but fine. You obviously are still here for a reason because you shouldn't be. Let me ask you a question. Do you remember anything that happened in the ambulance?"

"I remember hearing a voice, as I was coming and going in and out of consciousness."

Rising up very slowly from my seat, I began to walk around the room concentrating deeply on the car wreck and the time afterwards in the ambulance. "Yes, I think I heard a voice."

"Are you OK?" the doctor asked.

He asked me that question because I began to collect my personal belongings off a nearby table.

"Yes...Yes. I feel fine. Is it possible for me to leave?"

"Actually, it is...but only because we can't find anything wrong with you. You'll have to sign some papers for me. You'll also need to go by the business office to sign some additional paperwork. If you're going to leave so quickly, you should plan to really take it easy for a few days."

After signing the doctor's paperwork, I started toward the door but stopped and turned to face him.

"Let me ask you a question. What happened to the fellow who was in the car with me when the wreck occurred? He was a hitchhiker I'd picked up on the side of the road just minutes earlier. I asked the nurse, and she told me there was no one else in the car."

"I received no information from the EMTs that there was a passenger riding with you. You must just be imagining that, as a result of the trauma and the period of time you were unconscious."

"I had to ask. It's so real I can hardly imagine I was by myself. Thank you for taking care of me. I'm really glad I'm not seriously hurt and am being allowed to leave. My girlfriend should be here any time to take me back to my apartment."

I walked over and extended my hand to the doctor. He took my hand and gave it a firm shake.

"You're welcome. Go home and relax. You're going to be sore all over, I'm sure. You've had a very stressful day. I've never seen anything like this in my entire career. I'll say again that what happened to you today was nothing short of a true miracle."

I reached the hospital lobby deep in thought. Just as I got there, Abby entered through a side door. On seeing her, I reflected on what a beautiful lady she was, still in her early thirties with shoulder-length, dark brunette hair. I was never so glad to see her.

Immediately, she spotted me and rushed over to give me a big hug. I could tell she was distraught and nervous, not knowing the extent of my injuries. She quickly released her hug but continued holding onto my right arm.

"Oh, my God, Honey. Did they release you already?"

"Yeah, I just have to sign a few papers in the business office, and then I'm out of here."

Abby reached up and rubbed my face with one of her hands. "Poor baby, are you sure you're OK? You look terrible."

I took her hand, closed my eyes for a couple of seconds and then kissed it. "Yes, I'm fine. Shook up, but I'm fine. Especially right now, after seeing you." Smiling, I let go of her hand. "Let me sign the papers, so we can leave."

I walked to the business office and asked for the papers. Abby remained seated in the lobby. She got her cell phone from her purse and dialed a number.

"Hey, Marty, I'm at the hospital. Yes. He's pretty banged up, but actually in really good shape after such a severe accident. They've told him he'll be fine. At the moment, he's checking out and signing his release papers. This is all so hard to believe. Look, I left so quickly I forgot to tell you I put a copy of the governor's speech to the Doctors' Association on his desk. Would you please remind him about our nine o'clock meeting in the morning? Thanks."

I walked up to Abby, just as she was finishing her call.

"OK, I'll tell him," she said. "See you."

She put her cell phone back into her purse. Getting up from her seat, she took my hand. "Marty told me to tell you to hang in there."

"Let's get out of here!"

Chapter Five

Abby and I left the hospital holding hands. Nothing was said while we headed to the car, even though she kept looking over at me as we walked along. She punched the unlock button on her remote. It beeped, but she stopped just before getting in.

Looking intently at me, she asked, "Are you OK? I mean really OK?"

"I don't know," I said, looking into the distance.

We both got in her car, she started it, and we drove away.

"What do you mean, you don't know?"

"So much has happened today that I really don't know what to think. I just need some time to process everything and get back to normal."

"Yes, I believe you're right. Let's just give you some time. It's good the doctor confirmed there's nothing seriously wrong with you physically."

"Abby, please take me by the dealership on the way back to my apartment. I want to see the car. I'm sure it was taken there. I also need to find my cell phone, if it's still in the car."

"OK, but we won't stay long."

Pulling off the interstate and entering the front of Buddy Victory's dealership, Abby drove to the far side at my suggestion. I figured the open area on the right side of the building was where the wrecker would have taken my 350-Z.

"Oh, my God! There it is."

Abby pulled up close, parked, and we both just sat and stared.

"Please tell me that's not my demo."

"Gary, I don't see how you survived that. Look. Just look at it."

"God, this is unbelievable."

I pulled on the latch of Abby's car door and started to get out. She quickly grabbed my forearm. "No. Don't. Stay here. I know you want to get closer, but I don't want to. I can't stand to see any more."

She began to sob. I took her hand in mine and leaned over toward her. "Honey, are you going to be alright?"

After a long pause, she replied, "No, I'm not. Because I now realize you shouldn't be."

"Shouldn't be what?"

"You shouldn't be OK." Staring straight at the car, she pointed and said, "Look at that." Then turning back to me, she said, "You shouldn't have survived that accident."

She began to cry uncontrollably. There was a long pause as she struggled to regain her composure.

"Let's get out of here, please," she said.

"Yeah, let's go."

We drove out the entrance, and she looked over at me with tears still in her eyes.

"What are you going to do now?" she asked.

"I'm not sure, but I have to find a number."

"You have to find what?"

"A number."

"What do you mean…a number?"

"All I know is, for some reason, I have to find the number 89, and somehow it will explain much of this to me."

Abby said, "Gary, you are making absolutely no sense to me."

"Hon, just give me some time to sort all of this out, and I'll be OK."

At that, I took her right hand in mine, kissed it, and looked out my window, deep in thought. All I could think about was the voice I'd heard in the ambulance. *Find the number 89… what in the world did that mean?*

CHAPTER SIX

The next evening, I went to the YMCA located close to my apartment for a light workout. I wanted to get some of the stiffness out of my body. There were a few bruises in various places, but mostly I was just very sore and stiff.

I tied my tennis shoes while sitting on a long bench in front of a string of metal lockers. As I got up, my body hurt all over. It brought a slight grimace to my face.

Leaving the locker room, I walked up a set of stairs into the lobby and then immediately entered a large workout area. I picked up a towel from a table, draped it over my shoulders, and wrapped part of it around my neck.

Glancing up, I stopped abruptly. Taken by surprise, I realized I was standing directly behind a big man on a Stairmaster machine. He was wearing a white football jersey with a big number 89 on the back. The name 'JIM' was stitched above the numbers and ran across the back of his shoulders.

I couldn't help but move forward toward the man. Standing behind the Stairmaster, I leaned inward and asked, "Are you Jim?"

Without turning around, the man calmly said, "Yeah, and you're late."

I moved to the front, so I could look directly into his face. "Excuse me? How am I late?"

"I know your routine. You're always here by seven o'clock in the evening. It's now twenty minutes after seven. Well, at least you found me. So, how are you doing?"

That blunt question agitated me, so I replied, "I don't know. Who are you?"

"In due time, Gary. I guess yesterday's accident was no fun?"

"Fun? No, it wasn't fun at all. I was almost killed. I should be dead right now. And, by the way, how do you know about it?"

Jim ignored my question and asked, "Have you seen the car?"

"Yes."

"Scary…huh?"

"That's not the half of it."

"I did a good job, didn't I?" asked Jim.

"What in the world do you mean?"

"You're alive, and you're not seriously hurt. I'd say I did a good job of looking out for you. Wouldn't you agree? Considering how the car ended up, you did OK. I know you're sore, banged up a little…but nothing like the car. At least I got your attention."

"YOU got my attention? What did you have to do with it? And…attention for what? I almost bit the dust. A very hot car is now just twisted steel. And, I've got to pay the deductible on it."

"At least you're alive to do it. Besides, I didn't ruin the car. I protected you. Cars can be replaced. You, on the other hand...well...we didn't think you'd be so easy to replace."

I asked, "We? Who's we? And really, what are you talking about? Wait a minute. That voice. You. You're the voice I heard in the ambulance, aren't you?"

"Yes, I am. I'm also the hitchhiker you picked up before getting on the interstate."

"I recognize you now. You were wearing those dark sunglasses and a hat when I picked you up. You're both of those people? How can that be?" I asked. "How come I only heard you in the ambulance and didn't see you?"

"You had too much going on already...too much distraction. When you're in that kind of situation, your hearing is your strongest sense. I had to first protect you during the car accident, then get your attention in the ambulance."

Pointing to himself, Jim added, "Hey, I'm no rookie. Trust me, I know what I'm doing. Always remember that."

"I don't understand anything that's happening, but if you were somehow involved with my accident, did you have to start off by almost killing me?" I asked.

"You were never in any danger. I just had to get your attention."

"I'd say that's an understatement. So...can you tell me why the wreck happened?"

"You had the wreck...for a reason. So, later on you could tell other people."

At that, I said, "What?"

"Just listen. Life as you've known it is over. It no longer exists. You survived for a reason. Over time you will come to understand. From this point on, you're going on a very interesting journey into a totally different world. You're going to learn things about yourself that you never knew existed...stuff that's always been deep inside you. You just didn't know it."

"What are you talking about?"

"For one thing, you're well aware that you're a gifted, talented man. Your problem is that you're very self-centered, egotistical, selfish, and not to mention...arrogant. Believe it or not, in this life it's not all about you. That's the first thing you need to learn."

"Excuse me? Where did all of that come from? Why are you so on my case?" I asked.

"You think your gift is for you...and you only. But you're going to find out differently. You've got to learn your gift is not about you or for you. It's about...and to be used for, other people. Helping people, reaching people...touching people. It's all got to come from the heart. A gift is about giving... getting outside of yourself, which you know nothing about. But, you're getting ready to learn, and I'm going to teach you. Believe it or not, *life is not about making money. It's about making a difference*."

"So, what gift are you talking about?" I asked.

"It's something you do every day...and have been doing for years. Except now, you're going to do it for others."

I said, "Yeah, my gift is selling cars."

"No sir. It's shining shoes."

"What?" I said. "Shining shoes?"

"Yep. Shining shoes. Your gift is shining shoes."

"No, my gift is selling cars," I repeated again.

"Selling cars is something you're very good at. A gift is something you do that's good for other people. Sometimes, when you sell a car, it's not good for the other people. Not good at all. Sometimes...your customers or their families get hurt. That's not a gift, that's a curse. When you do something and people get hurt, it becomes a curse," Jim said.

"So, how am I going to sell cars AND shine shoes?"

"You're not. You're going to stop selling cars and just shine shoes."

I looked at Jim with a questioning expression I could not avoid, trying to understand.

"You're going to make a difference...one foot at a time. You're going to touch some souls. Get it? Human souls, not shoe soles."

"Yeah, that's real cute. Touch some souls. You're kidding, right? You're telling me I'm going to stop selling cars and set up a shoeshine stand?"

"No, you're going to do it differently. You're not going to have a stand or a shop. You are going to go to them. You see, when you use your gift, you never know where it will take you," Jim said.

With a very serious and caring look on his face and his index finger pointed upward, Jim then said with great emphasis, "Always remember this. ***A man's gift makes room for him and brings him before great men.*** The best way for that to happen is for you to take your gift to others."

"And exactly where do you fit into all of this?"

"My job is to get you polished. Kind'a like you polishing the shoes. We have to keep you on track to get you to where you're going. Don't underestimate your ability and who your gift might affect. *You never know whose shoes you may shine*."

Beginning to feel the whole concept was too overwhelming or just crazy, I leaned back against the next Stairmaster and began to think about what I was being told.

"OK. Let me go through the details as I understand them. I'm going to quit selling cars and hit the streets of Nashville shining shoes, and you're going to keep me polished, humble, and on track. Basically, you're going to turn my life inside out. Does that about size it up?"

"Yep. Pretty much," Jim replied.

"You've lost your mind. You've lost your ever lovin' mind. I'm going to hit the streets and start shining shoes. Is that right? I'll never make enough money shining shoes to pay even half of my bills."

Jim responded, with a slight grin on his face, "Don't worry about paying your bills. This will all work out. Trust me."

"OK, so where am I going to do this?"

"At first, we'll keep it simple, doing it a couple of ways. You're familiar with car dealerships, and you already know a lot of salesmen. You can start by going to car dealerships and shining the salesmen's shoes."

"Whoa, whoa, whoa, whoa…WHOA. Now, I know you've lost your mind. I'm not going to quit selling cars… which is what I do best! And start shining the shoes of other car salesmen…which I've never done. They'll laugh me out of the dealerships. I'll be humiliated. I'm not going to lower myself. And for what? Oh, that's right. I've got this special gift that I have to deliver to somebody. No, no, no, no, no…NO."

Jim said, "I want you to be able to see what I see. Yeah, you're going down a different path, a path of real greatness. I know you can't see it yet. Eventually, you'll be able to see things like I do. Remember this also. ***When you see the invisible, you can achieve the incredible***. As I said before, you just have to trust me."

"Wait, you said there were a couple of ways for this. What's the other one?" I asked.

"We can have you shine shoes here at the Y."

"Here at the Y? Get out of here."

About that time, the director of the Y walked by.

Jim said, "Excuse me. Aren't you Bob Jennings, the director here at the Y?"

"Yes sir, I am."

"I'm Jim."

"Hello, Jim," he said, while shaking hands. "Nice to meet you."

"Didn't we used to have a shoeshine guy downstairs by the locker room?"

"Yes, but it's been a couple of years ago. He retired. Why?"

"Do you know Gary Neal, standing here beside me?" Jim asked.

"Hello. Glad to meet you. I've seen you in here a lot."

Jim then said to me, "This is Bob, the director here at the Y. He's the main boss."

Turning back to face Bob, he said, "Gary here is the best shoeshine guy around. He would do a great job replacing the other fellow who's no longer working."

"Really?" Bob asked me. "Do you want to shine shoes here?"

"Uhhhhhh…I don't know."

"Well, if you want to, come by my office sometime soon, and we'll talk about it." Turning to Jim and then to me, Bob said, "Good to see you, Jim. Nice to meet you, Gary."

"You too," I said.

Bob then moved in the opposite direction and walked away.

"Well?" Jim asked me.

"Hey, slow down, Hoss. You're jumping the gun. I haven't said I was going to do this yet. Besides, my girlfriend would think I've lost my mind."

"Abby's not going to think you're crazy," Jim said.

"How do you know her name? Have you talked to her?"

"Not yet. I'd prefer not to. But that's up to you."

"How do you know she won't think I'm crazy?"

"Because she loves you. But right now is not the right time for you two. You need to focus on doing what we've talked about. I know you've made plans with her, but once you focus on what you have to do, everything else will fall in place. Otherwise, it will fall apart."

"What will fall apart?" I asked.

"Your life. Remember…life as you've known it, is over. It no longer exists."

Exhaling hard, the confusion in my mind was overwhelming. I needed time to think about what was being said. I just needed time.

"Don't wait too long. Every second counts. Think about what we've talked about…just don't take too long." Patting me on the shoulder, Jim concluded by saying softly, "Talk to you soon."

Then, he turned quickly and walked out of the room. I was left standing beside the empty Stairmaster. I put the towel around my shoulders and leaned over the machine. I was speechless.

CHAPTER SEVEN

After having showered and dressed, I left the Y and walked outside to my parked truck. Getting in, I started it and drove slowly out of the parking lot. I had noticed earlier that the vehicle needed gas, so I pulled into a convenience store about a mile away. I put my credit card in the gas pump slot, punched the numbers, and started pumping gas.

As I looked to one side, there was an apparently homeless man. He looked to be in his 60s, sitting on the curb, and staring right at me. I looked away at first because his stare made me feel uncomfortable.

After about ten seconds, I looked back over at him. He was still staring. I looked away again and then looked at him once more.

He said, "How's it going?"

"Going very well. Thank you," I replied.

"Have you decided what you're going to do?"

"About what?" I asked.

"Shining shoes."

"EXCUSE me?"

"Are you going to shine shoes?"

Looking around, I couldn't see anyone else close by. The man slowly got up, walked over, and stood only a few feet away.

"There's nobody out here but us," he said.

"Were you at the Y tonight?"

"Nope."

"Then how did you know......?"

"Doesn't matter," he said, while halfway laughing and looking over at my truck. "You haven't driven this old beat-up thing in a long time. That wreck was pretty nasty, wasn't it? Jim knows how to get your attention for sure." Looking at me even closer, he asked again, "He does know how to get your attention, doesn't he?"

"Who are you?" I asked, getting a little agitated. "How do you know Jim? And how do you know the deal about me being told to start shining shoes?"

"I know it's a tough decision. But, you'd better do what Jim says. I mean, if the wreck didn't get your attention...hey, it's your call. But, if I were in your place," and he leaned in closer, "I'd choose the shoes."

After saying that, he patted me on the shoulder two times, turned and started to walk away.

"Wait a minute. How do you know about all this? What else did Jim tell you?"

The man just kept going.

"Hey, you can't just walk away."

He kept going and didn't look back. I was feeling very frustrated and all I could think was, *Well, I guess you can just walk away.*

Looking up and speaking to the sky, I said, "OK, Jim, enough is enough. Come on now. This is not funny." Speaking even louder into the distance, I finished the first statement with a sarcastic comment, "Jim. This is just great. Thanks for nothing."

I glanced back in the direction of the old man, and he was completely gone. *How did he move that fast?* I thought.

After returning the gas pump handle to its cradle, I got back in my truck, started the engine, and drove away totally confused.

CHAPTER EIGHT

The next morning, I drove to the Buddy Victory dealership, went in, and walked up to Sue at the front desk.

"Hey, girl."

"Hey there. How are you? That was a horrible accident. I saw the car outside. Are you feeling better today?"

"A little sore, but I'm OK."

I checked my message box, took out a few messages, and glanced at them as I walked to my office. After entering, I sat down at my desk. I laid the messages on top and looked over at the pending vehicle deal file. Picking up the phone, I called the receptionist.

"What time is Scott Hines coming in? OK, thanks."

Hanging up the phone, I looked over and was shocked by what I saw outside through my window. As I stood up, my head moved side to side trying to make sure of what I was seeing out on the lot. If I was seeing right, there stood Jim in the parking lot looking at an almost new BMW. He was wearing a white football jersey with the big number 89 on it, just like at the Y.

I thought, *Doesn't he have any other clothes?*

I walked quickly out of my office, through the front door, and directly toward Jim.

"No, no, no, no, you don't," I said, while rounding the corner. As I reached his side, I asked, "What are you doing here?"

"What do you think?"

"You can't come to where I work."

With a slight smirk on his face, Jim replied, "I'm already here. So...have you decided yet?"

"Hey man, we just talked about it last night."

"And I told you the clock was ticking."

I said, "Look, I don't know what's going on, and I don't know what your deal is, but you're crazy if you think I'm going to quit doing this," as I waved my arms around at all the used cars on the lot, "and go shine shoes." Pointing my finger directly at him, I then stated with some anger in my voice, "And don't think you can 'tag team' me either."

"What are you talking about?"

"I'm talking about the homeless guy at the gas station last night."

"WHAT? A homeless guy at a gas station? What are you talking about?"

Getting even madder, I began to walk around in circles to vent my frustration. "Oh, yeah. Play dumb. You know exactly what I'm talking about."

CHAPTER NINE

Inside the dealership, looking out from the lobby window, three salesmen were standing and watching me move around erratically, as if I were talking to someone.

"How long has he been out there?" asked the first salesman.

"About five or six minutes," the receptionist responded from across the room. "He passed by here almost running. He went straight to the BMW and started acting very strange."

The other two salesmen started to laugh, but stopped and continued to watch what was going on outside.

One of them asked, "Man, what's up with him? Did the wreck affect his brain?"

About that time, Scott Hines walked up to the reception- ist. "What's happening?" he asked.

"That's what we're trying to figure out," answered another one of the salesmen. "We're talking about your friend. Check him out."

Looking out the window, Scott asked, "What's he doing? Is he talking to someone? There's nobody there. Who's he talking to?"

David Norton then came up and walked over to stand next to Scott. "What's going on?"

Pointing through the window, Scott said, "Look at Gary."

David stood silently, just observing my actions in the parking lot.

Sue picked up the phone. "Buddy, you need to come out here and see what Gary's doing." She then hung up the phone and continued to watch through the window.

"Who is he talking to, if nobody's there?" asked David.

"Good question."

Buddy came around the corner and entered the room. He noticed everyone looking out the window. "What's going on, guys?"

"That's what we're trying to figure out. Gary's talking to somebody, but nobody's there," said Scott.

Buddy asked, "How long has he been out there?"

"About ten minutes. He's been doing that the whole time."

"Well, somebody go out there and find out what's going on, please."

"Come on, David, let's go see what he's doing," said Scott.

CHAPTER TEN

Scott and David went out the front door and walked toward where I was standing near the BMW. I was still talking to Jim when they walked up behind me. My back was facing them, so I didn't see them coming.

To Jim, I asked, "Why did you pick the activity of shining shoes...and why now?"

"Is everything OK?" Scott asked from behind and startled me.

"Yeah, everything's fine. Just talking to a...friend of mine. Jim, this is Scott Hines, and this is David Norton. Guys, this is Jim."

Scott and David looked at each other with confused looks on their faces.

"Jim...Jim who?" Scott asked, and began to look around the area.

"What? This is Jim, standing next to me." I said, turning

around to face Jim. Pointing to him with an intense look on my face, I asked, "Wait a second. Can you guys not see him standing right here?"

I kept pointing directly at Jim and couldn't believe they were not able to see him.

"No. We can't see anyone," said Scott. "You seem to be by yourself, old boy."

"You don't see a guy standing right here?" as I waved my hand right in front of Jim. "This guy…wearing a white football jersey with the number 89 on the back of it. He's about six-feet-four and probably weighs around 250 pounds. You're telling me…you don't see him?" Waving both my hands and getting angry. I said, "He's right here, guys."

"Of course, we don't see anybody, because nobody's there," Scott said.

I began to look into Jim's face, feeling angrier by the moment. To Jim, I said, "You've got to be kidding. Is 'now you see me, now you don't' what we're playing?"

"Pretty much."

"There. Did you hear that? What he just said?" I asked Scott and David.

"Hear what?"

At that, I dropped my head to my chest and shook it from side to side. Looking back up at Jim, I asked, "Why are you doing this?"

"You know why," Jim responded.

"Why am I doing what?" Scott asked.

"I wasn't talking to you, Scott."

"What am I doing?" David asked.

"I wasn't talking to you either."

Scott asked, "Hey man, are you OK?"

"Yes, I'm fine."

Turning to Jim, I said, "See what you've done? My friends think I'm crazy."

Twisting around to face both Scott and David, I said, "I'm not crazy."

"You're now talking to us, right?"

Turning back to face Jim, I said, "See?"

Looking at David, who was obviously concerned about me, Scott asked, "See what?"

I could only close my eyes and drop my chin to my chest in total frustration.

"Hey Gary, why don't we go inside? It's kind'a getting hot out here."

"You guys go ahead, and I'll be there…in just a minute."

"Are you sure you're alright?" David asked, out of a real concern for me.

"Yes, David. I'm fine." Gaining just a bit more composure and calming down a bit, I repeated, "I'm fine, really."

Scott and David looked at each other as if they didn't believe me.

"Really guys, I'm OK. If I were NOT, you know I'd tell you. Look, I'll be inside in a minute."

"OK."

Scott looked over at David, tilted his head as if to say "Let's go." Then, they walked slowly into the dealership.

"Great," I said. "Do you have any idea how big an idiot you just made out of me?"

"You could make this a lot easier," Jim said.

"Why me?"

"Because…no one else has your gift. Not like you do."

"What is the big deal about this gift? You mean shining shoes, right? Why are you making such a big deal about me shining shoes? I've been shining my own shoes for years. Why do I have to go out and start shining other people's shoes? Why now?"

"Eventually, you'll understand why. And the sooner you get started, the sooner you'll get to the why."

CHAPTER ELEVEN

As Scott and David entered the dealership, Buddy was still standing near the window and asked, "So, what's the deal?"

"According to Gary, he was talking to a guy named Jim, who was wearing a white football jersey with the number 89 on it."

Buddy said in amazement, "You're kidding!" Then he asked, "Did he say what the guy looked like...other than that?"

"Oh, yeah. Six-feet-four...weighs about 250."

At that, Buddy closed his eyes and shook his head. "Something has happened to our boy."

"What do you think we should do?" Scott asked.

"I don't know if there is anything we can do," said Buddy, as he closed his eyes again and slowly shook his head. "Something has definitely happened."

I walked back inside, as they watched me enter the dealership's front door. Everyone was standing in a tight cluster and just staring directly at me.

Instantly feeling very uncomfortable, I thought to myself, *Great...what's next?*

Buddy asked without hesitation, "Are you OK?"

Getting agitated, I replied, "Yeah, I'm perfectly fine. Thanks for asking."

As I passed Buddy and the others, Buddy asked, "Why don't you step into my office for a moment?"

I stopped and looked Buddy directly in the face and said, "Buddy, I said I'm fine. OK?"

Walking toward his office, he repeated, "Come on. Let's talk."

I turned around to the others still standing in the lobby who were staring at me and said in a frustrated voice, "Guys, I'm fine...Really!"

With that, I followed Buddy into his office. He sat down in his chair behind his desk, and I remained standing in front of him.

Buddy took a deep breath and looked as if he were trying to decide what to say to me. "Were you talking to somebody out there a few minutes ago?" he asked.

Hesitating and clearing my throat, I replied, "Yes sir, I was."

"Who?"

"A guy named Jim."

"What did he look like?"

Hesitating even more, I answered him by saying, "A big guy...with brown hair, white football jersey with an 89 on it." Looking off to the side before going on, because I knew it all sounded crazy, I added, "About six-feet-four, 250 pounds."

"You saw this guy, out there on the lot?"

"Yes."

"How come no one else did?"

"I don't know."

"But you saw him…just like you see me? Right?"

"Yes sir."

With that said, I began to look to my left, through Buddy's window facing the other side of the lot. I could see Jim leaning back on my wrecked demo with his arms folded. He saw me watching, raised his arm and tapped his watch.

I reacted by gesturing with my hand and mouthing the word, "What?"

Buddy walked over to the window beside me and looked outside. He then turned, faced me and asked, "Do you see Jim now?"

"Yes. He's standing right out there leaning against my wrecked car."

Sitting back down at his desk, Buddy's reaction was for him to clear his throat, lean forward toward me, and cross the fingers on both of his hands. I could tell he was uncertain about what he should say.

"I think you need to take some time off. Go see a doctor."

"Why?"

"Because you're seeing a six-foot-four guy, wearing a white jersey with the number 89 on it…that no one else sees but you."

"Buddy, I'm not crazy."

Looking out the window again, I saw Jim motion with his hand to hurry up. I reacted by giving him the 'out' motion with my thumb, like an umpire does. Then, with gritted teeth and beginning to feel angry, I mouthed the words, "Get outta here."

Very matter-of-factly, Buddy said, "Gary, you're talking to someone nobody sees but you. Think about it. Something obviously happened to you in the wreck. Just take some time off, go to the doctor and get checked out."

I asked, "So, is this your slick way of firing me?"

"No sir, your job will be here when you come back. Just take some time off to find out what's going on."

"I don't need time off. I need to work."

Gesturing with his hand toward the outside, he said, "Gary, you were out there on the lot talking to somebody, but nobody was there. I saw you myself."

"There WAS somebody there…a guy."

At the same time, both of us said the same thing, "Named Jim."

"There is no guy named Jim."

"Yes, Buddy, there is. Trust me."

Looking out the window, Jim was still leaning back against the wrecked car with his arms crossed, just staring at me.

I turned around and faced Buddy, realizing the conversation was going nowhere and calmly said, "OK, I'll take some time off."

"Promise me you'll find out what's going on," Buddy said.

I looked back at Jim. He made a gesture by raising both his hands as if to say, "What are you going to do?"

I again looked at Buddy and said to him, "That's exactly what I'll do."

"Good. Take all of the time you need."

He tapped on his desk and stood up, ready to walk from the room. "Let me know if I can help," Buddy said.

"I will."

He extended his hand toward me with a slight smile on his face. We shook hands.

"Thanks, Buddy. You're a friend, and you're trying to help. I appreciate that."

I left his office and walked through the front door. Rounding the corner, I approached the wrecked demo. Jim was gone. I looked around and then yelled, "Hey, Jim. Would you please make up your mind? Hello??? I'm here!"

Inside, Buddy was looking out his window and staring at me. He was positive there was no one there and that I needed some serious help. He closed his eyes and just shook his head one more time.

CHAPTER TWELVE

Early the next day, I decided to stop by the Dimples Diner to get some breakfast. When I got out of my truck, I purchased a copy of the daily newspaper from a metal box located beside the front door. The paper was tucked under my arm as I went inside and sat down in one of their booths near the cash register.

I was busy reading the headlines when a big busted waitress, who looked a little like Dolly Parton, walked over to my table. She said, "Good morning!"

"Good morning to you."

"How are you doing today?"

"I'm OK, thank you."

"Good," she said. "Have you decided yet?"

"Oh, I'll have two eggs over easy, sausage, toast, and orange juice."

"Actually, I meant, have you decided what you're going to do?"

I had to stop and think for a moment about what she'd just said. My reply was, "About what?"

"About shining shoes."

That took me by complete surprise. I looked directly into her face and quietly asked, "How do you know about that? Who are you?"

"My name is Angel."

"Excuse me? Did I hear that correctly?" I asked.

"Angel. Yes, you heard me correctly."

"Let me get this straight. Your name is really Angel. Right?"

I looked away and shook my head in frustration. Speaking as if I were almost talking to myself, I asked, "How long is this going to go on?"

"Well, Gary. That's entirely up to you."

Again, looking at her, I tapped the fingernails of my right hand on the table top repeatedly, out of nerves and frustration. "How many of ya'll know my name?"

"All of us," she said, while smiling and continuing to stare.

"Obviously, ya'll don't give up."

"Not till you give in," Angel said.

With agitation in my voice, I could feel myself beginning to get a little upset. "So, I'll keep having these 'pow-wows' until I surrender. Is that the way it works?"

Smiling wider, she said, "Heeeeeeey, you aren't as slow as Jim said you were."

"What was that?"

"Don't get mad at me. I'm just a messenger," obviously trying to calm me down. "Waitresses make perfect messengers."

"You're not a real angel, are you?"

"Lord no, Honey. I'm a talker, not a fighter. I just show up and give the messages for the other guys. Maybe someday I'll make it to another level."

"So, you're here to give me a message?"

"Yes sir. You've arrived at the bottom line."

"OK. Let me have it."

"Here goes...I know it's a hard decision, but it's like Jim said. You can't see things like we do. There's something real big out there waiting for you. But, it's the shoes that are going to take you there. Not your shoes, but other people's shoes. Honey, believe me, it's big. Taking care of other people's shoes is going to take you places you can't even imagine. I know it's hard to do, but you've got to believe in something you can't see right now. And the more you give your gift away, the more you'll see what we're talking about. Trust me. You'll be able to see, through your gift."

"You mean shining shoes? Right?"

"Yes. That's where it begins. And, since you aren't working, now is the perfect time to start."

Giving her what had to be a frustrated look, I asked, "Do all of you know everything that's going on in my life?"

"Of course we do. Some of what's going on is our doing. You'd be surprised how many of us are watching out for you."

"Based on things that have occurred lately, I probably wouldn't."

She then said, "Listen. Don't take too long. The clock is ticking."

As she walked away and moved around the corner out of my sight, another waitress came up to my table. She laid a menu in front of me.

She said, "I'm sorry you had to wait so long. As you can tell, we're slammed this morning. There are a lot of extra people eating here today."

"That's OK. The other waitress took my order a few minutes ago."

Looking puzzled, she said, "What other waitress?"

"Angel."

"Angel? Who's Angel? I'm the only one here today."

Closing my eyes and shaking my head, I realized fully what had happened.

"Never mind…I'll have two eggs over easy, sausage, toast, and orange juice."

Picking up the menu, she said, "OK," and walked away.

Dumbfounded, I stared out into space and again shook my head from side to side.

CHAPTER THIRTEEN

After finishing breakfast, I went back to my apartment. I watched the sports channel on TV for a short time and later decided to make a phone call to my dad. Using the remote, I turned down the volume on my TV and placed the call.

"Hey, Dad. How ya doing?"

"Hello, son. I'm doing fine. Haven't heard from you in a while, and I was wondering how things were going."

"Not so good. I had a car wreck. Actually, I totaled my new demo."

"Oh, my gosh, I'm really sorry to hear that. Were you hurt?"

"No. I was by myself. No one else was hurt in the accident. I'm sore, but nothing was broken and no other problems. I was extremely lucky. Listen, I need you to do me a favor. I need you to build me a shoeshine box."

At that, I had to stop and laugh because I was sure it would take my dad by complete surprise.

"Yeah," I said. "A shoeshine box. I'm thinking about driving up to see you this Saturday. I'll explain it all when I get there. Would it be possible for you to make one for me by Saturday?"

"Sure, I'll be glad to do that, but I don't understand what you want with a shoeshine box."

"Dad, we'll talk more about it when I get there."

"OK, whatever you say. I'll have it ready by ten o'clock that morning. I'm so happy you weren't seriously hurt in the accident."

"Thanks, Dad. I'll explain everything when I see you, OK? I'll get there by ten. Love you. Bye."

Holding the telephone in my hand and rubbing it against my forehead, I closed my eyes for several seconds and thought about the things I'd experienced in the last few days before setting it down. Lifting my keys off the side table, I went out the door to my truck.

I drove quietly to the Buddy Victory dealership in deep thought. When I entered through the front door, the receptionist began to stare at me.

"Hey, Sue. How are things going?"

"Heeeey. Good to see you. The question is, how are you doing?" With her right hand, she gave me a 'so-so' sign, just checking to see if that fit the mood.

"I'm getting better."

"Good. Hang in there," she said. "Here are some messages for you. I was wondering if you'd be in today."

She handed me about ten messages with a few on top marked 'urgent.' I walked directly to Scott Hines' office. He was on the phone, but waved me to come in and have a seat. I put the messages in my front pocket and sat down.

While on the phone, Scott said, "Tanya, I gotta go. Gary just walked in. He looks like there's something important we need to talk about. Yes, I'll tell him. Love you, too."

Hanging up the phone, Scott got up and shook my hand. He told me to take a seat in a chair in front of his desk.

"Well, 'Crash,' Tanya says hello. How are you doing?"

"I'm OK, but I've been better."

Scott sat back down and said, "Yeah, I'm sure you have. That car was really messed up in the wreck. Whewww! Kind'a scary. Buddy said your tests indicated nothing was broken, no damage was done." Pointing at my head, he then added, "I guess you got hit in the head, huh?"

With a slight laugh, I simply said, "Yeah." I knew what he meant by the comment.

"Well, man, you look like crap. How do you feel? Really?"

"Like crap...still. I guess I'll be alright, but I need a little time."

"When are you coming back?"

"I'm not," I said.

"What???"

"I'm not coming back."

"Stop it." Then laughing, he said, "Yes, you are. You're just pulling my leg."

"Nope. I'm not joking," I said.

"You are serious, aren't you? Why?"

"Well, I'm not sure how to explain it exactly."

"Give it a shot. I'm listening."

"I know you're going to think I've lost my ever lovin' mind, but hear me out. When I was in the ambulance, headed to the hospital, I heard a voice. The voice told me the wreck happened for a reason. It told me my life was going to change. Since then, I met a guy that seems to know all the answers. I don't understand any of it, but I'm not coming back to work."

I stopped talking for a moment and let that sink into Scott's head.

He started talking again and said, "Wait a minute. You heard a voice. It could have been the EMT. Were you drugged up?"

"Maybe they had given me something. I don't think I was drugged. But, I know what I heard. The voice was real. I know I heard an unusual voice."

"And because of that, you're going to quit? Did this 'voice' tell you to quit?"

"Not then, but later. I talked to this guy I just mentioned who seems to have all the answers."

"You've got to be kidding me. Tell me you're kidding."

"No, I'm not. I'm quitting today...as soon as I get to talk with Buddy."

"Wow! So, what are you going to do for a job?"

Following a short laugh, I said to Scott, "You're not gonna believe me, but...I'm going to start shining shoes."

Scott leaned forward to make sure he was hearing correctly. With the fingers on both his hands intertwined and his elbows resting on the top of his desk, he asked, "Could you say that one more time? I'm sure I didn't hear exactly what you just told me."

"You heard me correctly."

"You're going to quit selling cars…and you're going to start shining shoes instead?"

Glancing around the room and then looking up, Scott followed that question with another one. "OK. This is a prank for one of those shows on TV where the camera is hidden. Is that right?"

"It's not a joke, Scott. I'm very serious."

"But you told me you don't shine shoes for other people. Remember?"

"Yeah, I know. But that's gonna change. A lot of things are going to change."

"Is this real, man? You're totally serious, aren't you?"

"Yes, Scott. This time I am."

"So, when are you going to start this new enterprise?"

"My dad is building me a shoeshine box. I'm going to Kentucky to pick it up from him on Saturday. He lives only a few hours from here."

"You're quitting…just like that?"

"Actually, I think I'll be just beginning."

"So, where are you going to set up shop?" Scott asked.

"I'm not gonna have a shop. I'll take my shoebox and travel around to different places to do the work. I plan to start going by car dealerships and shine the salesmen's shoes."

Busting out with a laugh, Scott jokingly said, "That can't be the truth. Shining other people's shoes for a living is so totally beneath you."

"I'm also planning to go to the local YMCA where I've been working out for years. I'm hoping to be allowed to set up outside the locker room. There should be plenty of shoes for me in that spot, from businessmen and others who want their shoes to look good. I can shine them while they're exercising."

"When are you planning to start?"

"First thing Monday morning," I said.

"The Y and at car dealerships. Do I have this right?"

"Yep. That's pretty much it."

"What's your overall game plan?"

"I'll start every morning at the Y, stay there for a couple of hours, and then hit the dealerships. I'll go back to the Y around four o'clock for a couple more hours in the afternoon."

Scott looked at me with a crazy stare and shook his head in disbelief. "This whole thing sounds extremely strange to me."

Getting up and beginning to pace around the room, I said to Scott, "I know you can't believe I'm really going to do this. But, I think I am. Even though I can't explain it, I know it's something I have to do. I'm sure it doesn't make much sense to you, because I'm walking away from a lot of money here at the dealership. I just feel I may be walking into something bigger…maybe even better."

"Gary, why would you give up everything you know to do this? You're such a successful car salesman. You're the best."

Sitting down again, I said to Scott, "The truth is, I really haven't been happy for a long, long time. No matter how much money I made, it was never enough. No matter how many 'salesman of the month' plaques I got, it wasn't enough. I don't know…maybe this guy with all the answers is right. Maybe it's not about making money, being at the top, getting the praise. Maybe it's about making a difference in other people's lives...as my new friend has told me. I do know this. I'm alive, and I shouldn't be. You saw the car. I survived for a reason. Now, I gotta go out and find out why."

Scott responded, "I guess you gotta do what you gotta do."

He reached out and shook my hand. "Hey man, best of luck. So, I guess you'll be doing my shoes after all?"

With a smile on my face, I said, "Yeah, I guess I will. David Norton has also been trying to get me to shine his shoes for a long time. I'll be doing shoes for both of you guys before long."

He walked over and gave me a big hug.

I said, "Thanks. You've been a great friend."

"Always will be. See ya around. Take care."

Chapter Fourteen

I left his office and walked directly to Buddy's. Standing in the doorway with my hands in my pockets, I saw that he was on the phone.

"Yeah, just come in first thing tomorrow morning. Tell the receptionist your name and she'll page me. See you then."

Buddy hung up the phone, looked at me, and walked over to shake my hand.

"Heeey…how are you doing?"

"How do I look?"

"Hope you feel better than you look."

I laughed and said, "I do…believe it or not."

"When are you coming back to work?"

Sitting down in a chair in front of his desk, I answered, "I'm not."

"What?"

"I'm not coming back. I'm quitting."

"Why?"

"I'm gonna do something else."

"Wait a minute. Are you serious? You're quitting?"

"Yes."

Buddy laughed and said, "No, you're not. I know you're pretty shook up right now. Just take some more time to let the dust settle. You'll be fine. You just got thrown off the horse. You'll be back in the saddle in no time."

"No. I've thought about this, and it's something I gotta do."

"What is something you gotta do? Did somebody offer you more money?"

"No, Buddy. I'm getting out of the car business."

"What? To do exactly what?"

Looking to the side, a little embarrassed and hesitating, I finally said, "I'm going to start shining shoes for a living."

"You're going to do what? Shine shoes? Where?"

"I plan to start going to a number of different dealerships and shine the salesmen's shoes. And, I'll also go to the local YMCA, where I've been working out for years and shine shoes there. Buddy, I know it doesn't make any sense to you. I just came in today so I could tell you face-to-face. You can give all my deals that I've been working on to Scott Hines. He'll do a good job for you with them. I've got a pocket full of phone messages Sue handed me earlier that someone needs to respond to. Here, take them."

I gave Buddy all the notes and bits of paper.

"Shining shoes at car lots and the Y? This is really serious?"

"Yes. It definitely is."

"Our office manager has to hear this. Let me get Steve Barnes in here."

He then reached over and punched a button on the pager system resting on his desk. It broadcast throughout the dealership. "Steve Barnes, please come to Buddy Victory's office as soon as possible."

When he finished, he turned to me and asked, "What made you decide to do this?"

"Buddy, you just wouldn't understand."

Steve Barnes walked into the office about that time. He was a short man who dressed sharply. It was obvious he was very aware of his appearance because he wore a vest, bow tie, stylish wire-frame glasses, and his dark hair was slicked back perfectly.

Steve asked as he entered the room, "What's this I hear about you quitting?"

"Gary just told me. How did you know about it?" Buddy asked.

"Scott Hines told me only a minute ago." Looking at me, he asked, "Just like that...you're quitting?"

"Yep. That's pretty much the deal."

Buddy then leaned back in his chair and said, "Ask him what he's going to do."

"Scott said it was something about shining shoes."

"Can you believe it?" Buddy asked.

"When you had the wreck, did you get hit really hard in the head? You definitely won't make anywhere close to the money you're making here. You won't get to drive the cars you can here. What're you going to drive around in, your old truck?" asked Steve.

"Yeah. That's the plan."

He laughed loudly at that comment. He just couldn't understand my change of attitude.

"What about Abby? What did she say?" Buddy asked.

"I haven't told her yet."

To Buddy, Steve commented, "He'll be back. She won't let him quit. She'll set him straight."

To me, Steve said, "Please tell me you're not serious. You're the best salesman we've got, and you're going to quit to do something for a living that you've never done before…like shining shoes? You're too good for that."

"What do you mean?" I asked.

"I mean that it's way beneath you. You're actually planning to go out and shine other salesmen's shoes? Nope. It can't happen. You don't have it in you."

"I don't have what in me?" I asked.

"You don't have the nerve to ask the other salesmen if you can shine their shoes for a fee."

"I'm going to be at the local YMCA, too."

"Nope. I don't see it. You won't do it for long. What made you decide to try this in the first place?"

"You wouldn't understand."

As I got out of my chair, I turned and said, "I just know it's what I have to do."

I politely shook Steve's hand and asked him, "So, when I come by, am I doing your shoes?"

"I guess so. We'll see how it all works out," he said, just before leaving the room.

Buddy stood up from behind his desk and I shook his hand. He said, "Hey, I almost forgot. Here's your phone. They found it in the remains of the car."

"Thanks for remembering it, but, before I leave, one more thing."

"What's that?" Buddy asked.

"I want you to go outside and look at that wrecked car with me."

"Are you sure?"

"Absolutely. Come on, let's go."

We both left his office together and walked to the side lot toward the car. Buddy and I approached it to within a few feet. I just stood still staring at the mess of metal that was beat up and twisted.

"Nobody can believe you got out of that alive, Gary."

Looking intensely at Buddy, I replied, "Neither can I."

I walked over to stand beside the driver's door and looked inside. It made my legs weak just to again see the mangled mess. I closed my eyes and quickly moved my head, as if shaking off the feeling. Breathing out heavily, I turned toward Buddy.

"Are you going to be alright, Gary?"

"Yes, considering what might have happened, I'd say I'm doing good. Wouldn't you?"

"I agree."

"Buddy, thanks for everything. You've been a great boss. I really appreciate it."

"You've always got a spot here. You know that. And don't worry about the deductible. You've made me enough money. I'll take care of it. I'm just glad you're alive. Remember, if things don't work out…"

I held up my right hand to stop him from saying any more, took his hand and shook it, while patting him on his shoulder with my left hand. "Thanks, Buddy. You're a good man and a great friend."

Afterwards, I left the dealership and drove away.

Heading down the interstate in my old red truck, the radio was playing a song that fit the moment. It was titled, *The Best Is Yet to Come.*

I picked up my cell phone and dialed Abby's number. I was surprised the battery wasn't dead. She picked up after two rings.

"Hey, Hon. What are you doing? I know about you and your long meetings. Working late this evening?" I asked, laughing just a bit. "Would you like to get together for dinner? How about we meet at the Alexandian Restaurant not too far from you? Good. Around 7:30? OK, I'll see you there. Hey, take it easy on the governor. He's a good one. OK, I love you. Bye."

I ended the call and drove to my apartment to get ready for dinner.

CHAPTER FIFTEEN

That evening at the restaurant, I arrived a little early to get a good seat by a large window. It wasn't long before I saw Abby's car pull into the lot. She parked, got out, and started toward the front door. I waved at her and then quickly called her cell number.

She answered with a sweet voice, "Hello."

"Stop," I said.

"Stop?" she asked, standing not ten feet from the front door.

"Yes, just stand right there."

"Why?"

"Because I want to take a photo of your unbelievable beauty, the way you look tonight. Give me ten seconds."

I disconnected the call and immediately took a photo of her with my phone. She was smiling broadly and turned around twice to show off her pretty dress.

She then walked through the front door and approached our table. I got up, hugged, and kissed her on the cheek.

"Hey, pretty woman. You look stunning, as always."

"Thank you. You're looking better."

We took our seats after I pulled out her chair from the table and afterwards pushed it back in for her.

"Thanks for agreeing to come. Long day?"

"Yes. We had a long staff meeting. We covered the governor's schedule for the next three months. Some internal problems had to be dealt with, which I can't discuss."

Rolling her eyes, she said, "Men and their egos. I don't get it. What's the deal with men and titles?"

"What do you mean?"

Abby said, "It seems that when you give a man a title, it goes straight to his head, then his ego gets inflated. I just don't get it."

"Anybody in particular?"

"Oh…I don't want to think about it anymore. How was your day?" Abby asked.

I laughed, and about that time, the waiter stopped at our table and brought each of us a glass of water.

"Hello. My name is Tim. Can I get either of you something stronger to drink?"

"Water is fine for me. Thank you for asking," Abby replied.

"Are you ready to order?"

"Yes. I'll have the Caesar salad with blue cheese," she said.

"I'll have the same." *I have to admit, I wondered a moment about Tim.*

The waiter wrote our order on a notepad and left to go back to the kitchen.

"Again, let me ask the question. How was your day? Did you work today?"

"I went to the dealership, but I didn't work."

"Did you get another demo?"

"No, I won't be getting another car."

"You mean Buddy's not going to give you another demo to drive because of the accident?"

"I'm not getting another car because I don't work there anymore…I quit."

"You quit? What do you mean you quit? Today? You quit today?"

"Yes."

"Why? You really quit? Why?"

"That's the reason I wanted to see you tonight. So I could tell you everything."

"Tell me what?" Abby asked. "Did they find something in your tests that you haven't mentioned? Is something wrong?"

"No…physically I'm fine."

"What do you mean physically?"

That question made me start fidgeting. Trying to collect myself, I stopped talking and took a drink of water.

"When I was in the ambulance, something happened. They told me I went 'on hold.' All my vital signs stopped for over five minutes. During that time, I heard a voice."

Just as that was said, the waiter came up to our table with the two salads and placed them in front of us. I was bothered by the interruption and paused for a moment to gather my thoughts.

To the waiter, Abby said, "Thank you."

To me, she asked, "You heard a voice??"

"Like I was trying to tell you, when I was in the ambulance, something happened. I'm not exactly sure, but they say I went 'on hold.' I heard this voice...a man's voice. He told me the wreck had happened for a reason. He said there was something I needed to find when I got out of the hospital...a number. When I talked with you the other day... remember? That was what I was saying I had to find. And I found that number."

"You said you had to go find the number 89," Abby remembered.

"That's what the voice said. I found a guy at the Y wearing a football jersey with the number 89 on his back. We had an interesting conversation, and he explained things to me."

With a mildly frustrated and even puzzled look on her face, Abby slowly shook her head and said, "What? Wait a minute. A voice in the ambulance told you to find some random number and you later talked to some guy with that number on his back?"

"Yes."

"What else did the voice say?"

"The voice said that once I found that number there would be answers to my questions."

"You found a guy wearing a football jersey with the number 89 on it?" Abby repeated with a bit of sarcasm in her tone. "What...no wings underneath it?"

She then took a drink of water and sat back in silence to think about what was just said.

"Come on, Abby. You don't have to be like that. I know it sounds weird, but it really happened. Besides, I actually found the guy, and he somehow knew everything about me."

With that, she stared at me with disbelief in her eyes. "You're telling me that you met this guy for the first time, and he actually knew all about you?"

"Yes."

"When?"

"The day after the wreck."

Leaning forward toward me, she raised her voice and said, "You met this weirdo...face-to-face?"

"Please lower your voice," I quietly said. "Yes, face-to-face." Abby took another drink of water, trying to settle herself. "I had a conversation with him."

"You talked to him?" she said, with an edge in her voice.

I closed my eyes for a moment and then looked around to see who might be listening. "Abby, calm down."

"Calm down? You're telling me you met some stranger with a mystery number on his shirt, had a conversation with him, and he told you to quit your job. How do you expect me to react?"

"I don't know."

"Let me understand this fully, he actually told you straight out to quit your job?"

Pausing for a few seconds before answering, I finally responded, "Yes."

Abby quickly crossed her arms and sat back in her chair. She stared at me with a very strange look. "Tell me you're kidding."

Getting a little irritated at her tone, I said, "This is not a joke. Do you think I would make this stuff up?"

"I don't know what I think right now." After a slight pause, she asked, "Since you quit, what are you planning to do now?"

I took a drink of my water, squinted my eyes shut, and tried to decide what to say next.

"Do you know what you're going to do?"

I hesitated. Abby smiled, and I was sure she was anticipating something better.

She asked, "Well, what?"

Looking down at the table, I responded quietly, "I'm gonna start shining shoes."

"What? That makes no sense at all. You've got to be out of your mind."

"I get your surprise, but I'm serious. I'm going to start shining shoes for a living."

"Shining shoes?" She started laughing. "You're going to set up a shoeshine stand and shine people's shoes?"

"No. I'm not going to have a stand. I'm going to take a shoeshine box and go to various car dealerships...and the local YMCA."

"To car dealerships and the Y? The Y...where you work out?" She stopped talking and put her head in her hands. "I'm not believing this. Are you really serious? Look, I know the wreck shook you up. But, quitting your job so you can shine shoes? Don't you think that's a little drastic? All because of a conversation with this stranger who told you to do it? What exactly did he say?"

"One thing he said really got to me. *A man's gift makes room for him and brings him before great men.*"

"A man?" Abby asked.

"I think it's in the Bible and means anyone. But he said I have a gift and it's not about me, but other people. It's about reaching people...affecting them. It's about giving of yourself. I don't know. It just made a lot of sense."

"So, you're saying you had an epiphany that you're to polish shoes."

"Abby, you call it what you want. But I know what I know. And I know this is what I have to do. I also know I need you to understand...to be on my side."

"I'm not sure, Gary." She hesitated and looked very sad, "I'm not sure I can."

"Really?"

"I don't know if I can be there for you under these circumstances. It's just too strange. What am I going to tell people? What will they say?" Pausing briefly, she almost begged, "Please don't do this to me."

"This isn't about you, Abby. I'm not doing anything to you. I thought you said you loved me."

"I do love you."

"What do you mean by that? You love me as long as I'm successful and making lots of money and driving fancy cars... taking you to places like this."

"Stop it," Abby said.

"But, that's the truth, isn't it?"

"No."

"Are you going to go out with me in my old red truck?"

Her expression answered my question.

"Are you? You never thought about that, and what the nice cars meant to you. Did you?"

"No."

Abby paused and looked up at me with teary eyes. Then she lowered her head.

"Abby, look at me."

She kept looking down.

In a stronger voice, I asked her again. "Will you please look at me?"

Abby slowly raised her head and looked up.

"I need to know if you're going to be there for this new adventure."

Abby looked back down at the table. "I'm not sure."

Her statement hurt me greatly. I tried not to react in a negative way but was definitely frustrated and feeling vulnerable.

I then asked her, "So...you don't love me after all?"

"I do love you. I do. But...what I want for us is a normal life, not you chasing some strange fantasy. I can't base my future on what some person told you to do. Gary...I really do love you."

"No, you don't. You love what I seemed to be, and in that role what I could do for you, and what I could give you. You can't even look at me."

Turning away myself and pausing, in order to think through what I was about to say, I carefully responded. "Well, at least I know the truth. And now, you do too."

At that, Abby took a deep breath and spoke in almost a whisper to me. "Gary," she said, "you just don't understand."

Growing even more agitated by her comments, I pushed back from the table and said, "No, Abby. I don't think you understand."

Catching myself in mid-sentence, I calmed down a bit and released a long sigh.

"Look. I know this doesn't make much sense right now. But...I do know this. Because of the wreck, I shouldn't be here. I'm convinced I'm now alive for a reason. There's something big out there waiting for me. I just know it. And, when it happens, I want you there by my side. I want you to be a part of it. I want to share it with you. This guy...the one with the answers, said something that made me stop and think. He said, '**Life isn't about making money, but about making a difference.**' Abby, I've made money, and now I want to make a difference. I've been chasing 'stuff' for too long...'stuff' I really don't even want. Status...admiration. I'm tired of chasing 'stuff' that doesn't matter."

After saying that, I took a moment for it to all sink into her mind. Then, I started again.

"Whatever is out there, I want to know what it is. I gotta go find it. I have to. I just want you to be with me when I do. Abby, I want you there with me because I love you."

She looked at me with a sad expression on her face, and said in a low voice, "I want to be there."

"Why do I feel there is a 'but' coming?" I asked.

"Gary, I love you. And I want to be there...but...I have plans of my own." That was followed by another brief pause. Then, she started up again, "I have big plans."

Getting up from the table, there was an awkward moment of silence, as she reached over to try and take my hand. I was so hurt that I didn't let it happen.

She said, "I hope you find what you're looking for...I'm sorry. I'm really sorry."

After that final statement, she slowly walked across the room and left through the front door. I watched out the window as she got in her car and drove away. I was crushed and feeling about as low and alone as I thought I could get. As I sat there, I felt the tears in my eyes.

CHAPTER SIXTEEN

When Abby got into her car after leaving the restaurant, all she could feel was disappointment. She started the engine and turned on the radio to distract her mind. She heard the last part of a familiar tune and the words, "in the arms of an angel," before bursting into tears.

Her cell phone began to ring, so she turned down the volume on the radio. She looked at the phone and saw it was her mom calling.

With hurt feelings, she thought, *That's bad timing, Mom*, but answered the phone anyway.

"Hi, Mom," she said, as a little edge slipped into her voice.

After a slight pause, she spoke again.

"Yes. I'm doing fine. No, nothing's wrong." Another pause. "Okay...there is something wrong. Gary and I broke up tonight...just now. Actually, I guess I broke up with him. Well...something has happened to him since the wreck. He says he met a man who's convinced him to quit his job. That's what he did today. Yes…today. Are you ready for this? He's going to start shining shoes for a living instead of selling cars. Yes…you heard me correctly. He said this individual told him he has a gift that will take him to great men. Now…he's going on this journey, headed down some path…to somewhere. I don't know. It just sounds crazy. I do love him, Mom. You know I love him very much. I do want a life with him, but I want a normal one…not chasing some insane fantasy down some unknown path."

Abby stopped talking for a moment, as her mom made a few comments to try and console her.

Continuing, Abby said, "He just told me at the restaurant. Afterwards, I walked out and left him sitting there. No. I didn't say anything about my new job offer. I guess there's nothing to stop me now from taking that job. It won't matter that it involves moving out of town. It's an amazing opportunity, a truly important job I'd really like to do."

With that said, Abby began to cry again. It made her feel bad to do that while talking to her mother.

She said, "Mom, I need to go. I'll talk to you tomorrow. Don't worry. I love you. Bye."

Abby then hung up the phone, turned the volume on her radio back up, and continued to cry while driving home listening to the music. It was all so sudden, and so very, very strange. Everything was going to be different. The hurt was deep.

CHAPTER SEVENTEEN

I made it back home and lay down on my bed with all the lights turned off. Looking out the window, I noticed rain was coming down heavily outside. My radio had its dial positioned so it would pick up my favorite station.

The song playing was, *If It's Gonna Rain.* Its lyrics fit the night and my feelings. Lightning began to flicker in the distance as the melody and the words from the radio went through my mind.

I got up and walked across the room to stand in front of the window. Rain ran down the glass panes in long streams. I went back and kneeled beside my bed, pulled a box from underneath, and set it on a table. The lights were turned on, so I could easily see its contents. Inside were pictures of Abby and me. There was a stack of them. I laid them out on the table, side-by-side in rows, and just stared. Sentimental words from the song continued to flow from the radio.

Tears formed in my eyes, as I looked at the many photos. I picked up four of them, walked to my bed, and lay down in despair. The song continued.

My right arm moved over to cover my eyes. All I wanted to do was go to sleep.

CHAPTER EIGHTEEN

After a light breakfast the next morning, I got in my truck to go visit my dad. I drove through downtown Nashville on my way to I-65 North and then continued toward the Kentucky state line. All the time, I was thinking about Abby and everything that had happened. Was I doing the right thing? What a hole it was going to leave in my life by losing her!

It wasn't long before I saw a sign on the side of the interstate that read, *Welcome to Kentucky*. I knew I was getting close. Shortly afterward, I pulled into my dad's driveway, parked, and walked around to the back of the house. He was standing in his workshop, working on an old chair. Dad stopped, walked over to me with a huge smile, and gave me a big hug.

"Hello, Son. Glad you came to visit."

"Hey, Dad. It's good to see you."

"You got pretty banged up, I guess."

"Yeah, I did. Nothing serious."

"How do you feel today?"

"All I've got left is a little soreness and some bruises. I was very lucky. The soreness is slowly working its way out and almost gone. Otherwise, I'm fine."

"Have you been working?"

"No. Not yet."

"Buddy will be throwing a fit if you're not back at work pretty quick," he said.

"Well Dad, I don't work for Buddy anymore."

"What?"

"Yesterday, I told him I quit."

"You told him you quit? Why?"

"You're gonna think I'm crazy."

With that statement, he laughed and then showed a bit of his sense of humor. "I've always thought that, but that's what I love about you. That's what makes you…you."

Then he got a serious look on his face, cleared his throat and said, "So…let's hear it." He sat down to listen.

"When I was in the ambulance, on the way to the hospital after the accident, something strange happened. All of a sudden, they say everything stopped…my heart, my breathing, no blood pressure. It all stopped for over five minutes. I heard a voice…a man's voice. The voice said that I was going to be fine, and that the wreck had happened for a reason. The voice told me to find a particular number, and it would lead me to a guy who would give me answers about why the wreck had happened."

I stopped after that for a moment, picked up a piece of

wood off Dad's table, played with it in my hands and began to walk around the room.

Turning and looking him right in the eyes, I said, "I found a guy wearing that number in the Y where I go, and he knew all about me."

"You found who?"

"The guy I was told to find. He was wearing a football jersey with the number 89 on the back. That's what the voice told me to find...the number 89."

"At the Y? What was this guy doing at the Y?"

"Working out...on a Stairmaster machine."

"Hmm," Dad said, "Go on."

"We talked for quite a while. He told me my life was going to change...that I was going to change. He said I was going to stop selling cars and start shining shoes for a living."

At that, my dad began to laugh.

"You always did like shining shoes, didn't you? Remember when I taught you how when you were little? I'd have you do mine on Saturday nights for church on Sunday morning."

I had to smile as I remembered doing exactly as he had said. Many times, I'd shined his shoes after he had taught me how to do it correctly.

"Yeah. I used to love doing your shoes. I do remember you telling me how important it was to keep my shoes shined. It stuck with me. That's why I shined my shoes every day before our sales meetings."

Dad asked, "So...does this person have a name?"

"Uh...yeah. Jim."

"Jim?" Dad asked, with a puzzled expression.

"Yeah."

"Why did he tell you to start shining shoes?"

"He said it was my gift."

"Your gift?"

"Yeah. He told me, '**A man's gift makes room for him and brings him before great men.**' He explained that my gift of shining shoes would do that for me."

"So…he told you to quit selling cars and start shining shoes?"

"Yeah."

"What did Buddy say?" asked Dad.

"He tried to talk me out of it. But, overall, he handled it pretty well."

"Have you told Abby?"

Rolling my eyes and hesitating to give the answer, I finally replied. "Yeah."

"I take it that didn't go well."

"No. It's really sad. We're not seeing each other anymore. I told her last night when we went out for dinner. She tried to talk me out of it several times; asked me a lot of questions. I think she's afraid I'm going to embarrass her, throw away my life, and all my potential. She just got up and walked out. I haven't heard from her since."

"How are you doing with that?"

"Not good. But what can I do? Life goes on. Right?"

"Yes, it does."

I continued, "She pretty much thought I was crazy…taking the advice of a stranger that the voice in the ambulance led me to. Quitting my job selling cars…starting to shine shoes instead. I'm beginning to wonder if I'm really a little crazy."

CHAPTER NINETEEN

"Son, I'm going to tell you something I've never told any-body...not even your mother. It's a secret I've had since I was sixteen years old."

He stopped and cleared his throat before continuing. With great seriousness in his voice, he again started to speak.

"I came down with typhoid fever three months before turning seventeen. The prediction was that I was going to die. I heard Mama and Daddy, your Uncle Carl, and Uncle Bill talking to the doctor in the hallway outside my room. I could hear the doctor telling them there was nothing he could do. While I was listening to what was being said, I noticed a big man standing at the foot of my bed. He walked over to the side, leaned down, and told me not to listen to them. He said I was going to be sick for a while, but that I was going to make it. He told me I would find out later why I was sick. It had something to do with the fact I was going to meet and marry a special woman for a reason…your mother. I fell asleep, and when I woke up, he was gone. I'll tell ya, it was strange, and even scary."

"Wow! I'll bet. So…who do you think it was?" I asked.

"I think it was a very special person, like that Jim, who you've recently met…had to be."

"You're kidding…right?" I asked.

"Nope, I'm not. I've always believed that to be true."

"What happened? How soon did you get better?"

"Back then, it was near the end of the Korean War." He hesitated slightly before continuing. "Hardly anybody was left in Eddyville, Kentucky. After you graduated from high school, you either helped on the farm or you went into the Army. I wanted to stay around there, help my dad with the farm, and start a family. I wanted three sons. I got four. You were an extra bonus."

With that, he stopped talking briefly and patted me on the back.

"It took a long time before I got better. The illness kept me home. It kept me close to my dad. He really depended on me. He was getting pretty sick himself at the time.

"How so?"

"His heart. I could tell something was going on with Dad while I was sick. Right after I graduated, it seemed as if everybody went overseas. I stayed behind. I met your mother while I was recovering. Her mother was my nurse. They both took care of me. That's when we fell in love. From the start, I felt sure she was the woman this person had in mind that I should marry. She graduated two years before I did…went to nursing school. We got married a few months later."

I asked, "How did you end up in Madisonville?"

"They built a brand-new hospital there right after we got married. Your mom was offered a great job with a lot of promises. Somehow, I knew we had to go. I had a feeling that hospital would make a difference in our lives one day."

Dad paused again before going on.

"That's where you were born. When you were eighteen months old, you got meningitis. That was the only hospital around able to deal with meningitis at the time. Because your mother was in the first group they hired, and because of how long she had worked there, they came through on their promise and our medical care was free. You got so sick you should have died, but the doctor named Calhoun, that your mother worked for, was the best around at pediatrics. He worked hard to save your life. He tried everything. According to him, at one point, you were only about four hours away from leaving us."

My dad stopped, lowered his head and shook it while remembering those past events.

"I'd never prayed so hard in my entire life. I was in the hospital chapel praying and heard the same voice from behind that I had heard at sixteen. There were people in the chapel at the time, but no one standing close to me. Looking around, I saw the same guy I had seen at my bedside when I was so sick. He had this way about him of knowing what was going to happen in the future. Apparently, he could be either visible to others or totally unseen, whatever he chose to do, and he would appear at odd times. In my case, I could always see him clearly when we talked, but others couldn't. After he walked over to me, he told me not to worry…that you would make it. He said there were some big plans for you. Then, he slowly turned around and quietly left the chapel without saying another word. I don't think anyone else in there saw him; at least they didn't act like they did. About an hour later, Dr. Calhoun came out and said a miracle had happened. Your temperature had gone down, and you pulled through. I never heard or saw the man again after that day; the man who had reassured me."

My dad paused only briefly before going on.

"So…it looks like we're about to find out what that person was talking about, as far as you are concerned."

"It looks that way, Dad," I said. "My doctor at the hospital told me a miracle had happened after the car wreck. He said it was something he couldn't explain…I shouldn't have made it." I then asked my dad, "What was the man's name, the one who came to you?"

"Jim," he said.

"Jim? That's really odd. No last name?"

"No. Why is that odd?"

"I'll tell you in a minute. What did he look like?" I asked.

"He was a big guy…weighed somewhere between 240 and 250. Tall…about six-foot-four or so, with dark brown hair. What did you say was the name of the guy you found with the number 89?"

Hesitating, I replied, "Jim."

"What did he look like?" Dad asked.

Walking around the room, I began to think about what my dad had just told me. Slowly, I said to him, "He looked exactly the way you described the man you saw. But it can't be. What's really odd is that they both had the same name and looked exactly alike. I've got to think about all this a little more. At the moment, I don't know what to say. Where's the box you were going to build for me?"

Dad walked across the room and from behind a table pulled the box out and set it on top. I picked it up and looked it over. The box he had built was perfect.

"Cool. This is great. Did you have a pattern to go by to build it?"

"No. Well...I didn't completely do it all by myself."

"What do you mean?"

"Do you remember right after I retired? I started helping your brother Donnie in his wood shop. He was quite ill at the time. I really enjoyed working with him and asked him to teach me how to make some stuff. At first, he taught me how to do small things; a bread box, towel hangers for the bathroom, and a magazine holder to put beside the couch. He later took some scraps of wood and started making this shoe box."

"Yeah?"

"Donnie died a week after he started working on it. He was only halfway done. I always told myself I'd finish it."

"He had his heart attack a week after he started working on this box? Dad, that was almost four years ago."

"I know. I just couldn't make myself finish it. To have done that would have meant I had let go of him. I just couldn't do it."

Dad stopped talking. We just looked at each other. Then he turned away. Finally, he was ready to continue.

"When you called me and told me you wanted a shoeshine

box…well…I didn't know if I could finish it. Actually, it's been good for me. I realized I didn't have to let go to finish it for you. I would be passing it on. Donnie was very excited about building it. It was intended for you from the start. He told me while working on it that he was making you a shoe-shine box for Christmas."

Dad reached over and picked up the box.

"Your brother knew how much you loved to shine your shoes. He remembered the time you shined his shoes for a job interview. Do you remember?"

Nodding my head, I answered, "Yes."

"He couldn't believe the great job you had done. He said the guy giving the interview made a comment about his shoes after seeing them. Donnie was the last interviewed that day. The guy told him that anyone who took care of his shoes that well would surely take good care of his clients, too. After that, he was hired."

I said, "He never told me that."

"I know. He was going to tell you when he gave you the box at Christmas."

"That's amazing. Thanks for letting me know."

"So now, whenever you shine a pair of shoes, you've got both me and your brother with you."

I paused and thought about what my dad had just said.

"So…you don't really think I'm crazy, do you?" I asked.

"Oh. You're crazy alright, but not for doing this with the shoeshine thing. This is something you've gotta do. Actually, after knowing who you've talked to and all that has happened, you're crazy if you don't."

"I'm so glad you understand, Dad."

"Yeah. You gotta do this. I mean…think about it. Back in the day, I could have gone off to fight like everyone else in the war. Obviously, there was another path for me. My life was changed by my illness, all for the good of the family. If I hadn't stayed behind, I might not have married your mother. In that case, I wouldn't have you now. See?"

"Yeah," I said.

"And be careful who you listen to. Everybody said I was crazy for getting married so soon. They said I wasn't healthy enough to get married, much less start a family. My dad got mad and threw a fit. The only person who believed in me was your mama…and she was the only one that really mattered. You'll find out who's on your side and who isn't. You'll get a lot of advice, whether you ask for it or not. Just do what Jim tells you to do. When I got better and started feeling good, I found that out the hard way. I thought I could play around and date girls other than your mother, but as a result, I got real sick again. The doctor almost lost me a second time. I asked your mom to marry me in the hospital and immediately started getting better. When Jim gives you instructions, it's not negotiable. Don't ever forget that…ever."

After another slight hesitation, Dad continued.

"You're going to be OK."

He reached over, patted me on the back, and said, "I've got faith in you. The thing is, you've got to have faith in yourself. If you don't, it doesn't matter what others think."

"Yeah, you're right, Dad."

I put my hand on my dad's shoulder before embracing him

with a big hug. A few seconds passed before I could let him go. "Thanks, Dad. For everything."

He looked me in the eyes and said, "Now…go do what you've gotta do."

"I will. Thanks again. I love you."

With that, I picked up the shoeshine box, walked out the door, climbed into my truck and drove off.

CHAPTER TWENTY

On the way home, I passed a copy shop not two miles from where I lived. Taking a hard right, I made a U turn by turning around in front of another store and went back. The tires on my truck squealed as I pulled into the parking lot. Hopping out, I went into the business.

"Hey, there. Can I help you?" the store clerk asked.

"Yep. I need some cards printed quickly."

"You came to the right place for that."

"I need business cards for a shoeshine guy. I'll give you my name and phone number to put on them."

"Are they for you?" the clerk asked.

"Yep."

"You gotta be kidding."

"Why's that?"

"You don't look to be a shoeshine guy. Is this a joke?"

"Maybe, but I need the cards. What's the smallest quantity you can print?" I asked him.

"We can print 100 in about five minutes. Will that work?"

"Do it. I'll give you my information."

I wrote down my name and phone number on a piece of paper, and handed it to him.

"Mr. Neal. There are some misspelled words here."

"I know. That's the way I want them spelled. Read along with me what those words say. I can help you 'heel.' I'm good for your 'sole.' I'm willing to 'dye' for you. It's a play on words."

Smiling back at me and beginning to laugh, the clerk said, "Oooohhhh...I get it."

"That's just my sense of humor to get my point across, and by the way, can you print out a picture from a cell phone?"

"Yep. No problem. Do you have the phone with you?"

"Here it is. I'll show you the one I want. I need two of them printed in a three-by-five inch size."

"Cool. I'll have all of this ready for you in a few minutes."

He put the paper with all my information on it in a big envelope, wrote on the outside, and walked to the back of his shop.

I left the sales counter and moved to the front of the store. There was a reflection of me in one of the large windows by the side of the door. I checked my hat, suspenders and necktie. They were considered part of my standard 'look,' and some version had been worn every day.

Outside, I saw a 350-Z red convertible in the parking lot, just like the one I'd crashed a few days earlier. I began to stare at it. Visions of the recent car wreck went through my mind, so I looked down and away. Looking back up, the car was still there. Closing my eyes, I started to visualize myself sitting in it, unconscious with a bloody forehead, with Jim sitting in the car with me.

A moment later, I glanced back through the window and thought I saw Jim in the car. I blinked my eyes and figured my mind must be playing tricks on me.

The clerk said, "OK, Mr. Neal."

Because I didn't immediately respond, he repeated my name.

"Mr. Neal?"

"Yes," I answered, as I turned toward him.

"You're ready to go. I've got all your stuff finished."

I was a little confused with what I thought I'd seen in the parking lot, so I turned back to look again. The car was gone. It had just vanished.

"Whoa…that was crazy. I must have imagined it," I mumbled to myself.

I walked to the counter to get my cards, the photos, and pay the bill.

"OK, Mr. Shoeshine Guy. That will be $9.95 for the cards and 5 bucks each for the photos, plus tax."

I picked up the pictures and looked at them while the clerk was punching on a computer keyboard.

"Man, that lady in the picture is hot," he said. "Your total is $21.80 with tax."

I took out my wallet and handed him $25.00.

He asked, "Is that your girlfriend?"

"Well…she was my girlfriend. Keep the change."

"Thanks. I still can't believe the cards are for you. You just don't seem the type."

Laughing slightly, I replied, "Yeah. I know."

I picked up the two photos, my business cards, and started to leave the store. Just as I reached the front door, I turned and said to him, "Thanks. You did a nice job. Have a good one."

"You too," he said.

After exiting the store, I stopped and began looking around the parking lot for the 350-Z I thought I'd seen. But it was nowhere in sight. I took a deep breath, let it out, and climbed into my truck. *It must have just been my imagination.* One last time, I looked around the lot before driving away.

CHAPTER TWENTY-ONE

My boom box was blasting inside my apartment the next morning. It was playing a lively song, *On the Sunny Side of the Street.* I listened while getting ready for work. Looking in the mirror, I put on my suspenders and a nice tie. I intended to continue with my 'look.' On a coat rack in the corner was a black fedora hat that I loved. Without hesitation, I went over and got it, put it on, and went back to the mirror.

Yep. Lookin' good! I thought to myself.

I picked up the shoeshine box Dad had made and checked its contents to make sure everything I needed was inside. I taped one of the photos of Abby, made at the copy shop the day before, to the inside wall of the box. I thought being able to see her each time I got items out of the box would be nice. Once it was in place, I shut the box. But then, I opened it one more time and looked at her picture before closing it once more. From a small table near the door, I picked up my keys and slid them in my right pocket.

I locked the apartment and walked to my truck. I placed the shoebox in the passenger seat. Before starting the engine, I opened the lid again and took another long look at Abby's photo, then drove off with the goal of starting my first full day of shining shoes.

Moving down the interstate, I turned up my car radio to the max. Another good song was playing. I started humming to the melody of *Takin' It to the Streets.*

I hadn't driven two miles when I realized I needed to eat before starting to work. There was a new restaurant near one of the exits, so I pulled my truck off the road and into their parking lot, which was only half-full. After parking, I went into the restaurant with my shoebox in hand.

Just past the front counter, I placed my box on a stool and sat on another one next to it. I started to watch a television hanging on the wall in front of me. The waitress came over after about thirty seconds.

"Good morning. How are you today?" she asked.

"I'm just fine. Hope you're doing well, also. Coffee, please," I replied.

She got the coffee pot, walked back over, and poured me a cup.

"Thanks."

"Do you need a menu?" she asked.

"Nope. Just gimme two eggs over easy, bacon, and toast."

About that time, an older, African-American man walked up and sat down on the stool next to me. He seemed cheerful enough by the look on his face. He was impeccably dressed, wearing a dark, pinstriped double-breasted suit, white starched shirt, and a solid-blue power tie. His was the 'executive look.'

"Good morning," he said cheerfully.

Laughing, I tried to make a joke out of it that only I would understand. "If you say so," I replied, while continuing to watch the TV.

"I do say so. And I'll improve that by adding, it's a great morning."

The waitress walked over about that time to see what he wanted to drink.

To her, he said with a smile, "I'll just have some coffee and toast."

"I'll get those for you right away."

She got the coffee pot off a nearby counter, walked back over, and poured him a cup of coffee. Afterwards, she went to the kitchen to place the order for his toast.

He said to me, "So…why is this not a good morning for you?"

I shook my head and rolled my eyes, "It's a long story."

"Does it have anything to do with the box?"

"Actually, it has everything to do with the box."

"So, what's the box for anyway? Do you shine shoes?" he asked.

With a sarcastic laugh, I replied, "Yeah."

"Really? How long have you been doing that?"

"Today will be my first day. I haven't even started yet."

"In that case, it's a good time to get started." He swung around and looked down at his shoes.

"What do you mean?"

"I mean, I need a shine. I have an important meeting tonight. Where do you want to do it?" he asked.

"You're serious, aren't you?"

"Definitely." He pointed to a nearby table with four empty chairs and said, "How about over there?"

We got up and walked to the table. I put my shoeshine box on the floor in front of him and got the necessary items out. The man put one of his shoes on the top of my box, and I got started.

Our waitress soon brought our food and placed it on top of the table. She said, "You both moved on me." With a gasp, she added, "What the heck are you doing?"

I answered her by saying, "I'm shining his shoes," as I finished the first shoe and started on the second one.

"You're a shoeshine guy? I didn't know anybody still did that. As a matter of fact, I've never seen anybody do it."

"It's a dying art," my first customer explained. "These days, not many people get to see it done."

"Well...I think it's great. You'd better both eat before it gets cold," she said, before walking across the room to take care of another customer.

"It's been a long time since I've found anyone willing to do this for me."

"Really?"

"You just don't see this done much anymore. It's definitely a lost art. I'm glad to see you doing it. You know, **big things can happen to a man who's willing to do small things**."

Looking up and laughing, I said, "Yeah. That's what I've heard. So...what's your name?"

"Virgil."

"Virgillllllllll?"

While staring directly into my eyes, he repeated once more while smiling, "Just Virgil."

"OK."

"Nice to meet you, Gary." He said without hesitation.

With a surprised look on my face, I quickly asked, "How did you know my name?"

He ignored my question, looked down at his shoes while eating his toast, and asked, "Are you finished?"

"Uhhhh...yeah." I said, wondering if he was going to explain how he knew my name. I sat down in the chair beside him and began to eat my breakfast.

"How much do I owe you?" he asked.

"I don't know."

"You don't know how much you charge?"

"I don't. This is my first shine."

He said, "Well...come on now...everyone has his price. How does five dollars sound?"

"Five dollars it is."

He then handed me a ten-dollar bill and said, "Keep it."

"That's a ten-dollar bill."

"Yes, it is."

"I only said five dollars."

"Remember... **You're always worth more than you think you are**," he said, with a smile.

"Thank you. That's very kind. I can certainly use the extra money."

Looking down at his shoes, he said, "No. Thank you! You've done a really fine job. Have a great day."

Virgil then got up, went over and paid for his coffee and

toast, and walked out the front door. I was still wondering how he knew my name but had been so busy working and eating I hadn't taken the time to ask again before he left.

I finished my breakfast, put everything back in my shoe-shine box, paid for the meal and walked outside.

As I was getting in my truck, I took a moment to ponder what Virgil had just said. ***You're always worth more than you think you are****. What an interesting way of looking at things.*

CHAPTER TWENTY-TWO

After leaving the restaurant, I stopped at two different car dealerships where some of the salesmen were good friends. I told them about my recent job change. None of them could understand why I had made such an abrupt move, but readily agreed I could shine their shoes. They even introduced me to other salesmen I didn't know, which led to keeping me busy most of the morning. At first, it was a little embarrassing because I figured they wouldn't have any respect for a shoe-shine guy, but as time went on, I slowly began to feel more comfortable with what I was doing.

In the afternoon, I drove over to the Y. When I walked into the workout area, Jim was on the Stairmaster across the room with his back toward me.

I walked over and without him even looking around, he asked, "What's up?"

"Not much," I replied.

"Having fun?"

"I guess."

"Don't guess. Either you are, or you aren't. Are you?"

"Yeah...sort of."

He got off the machine, turned toward me, and gave a 'time out' signal with his hands. "OK. What's going on?"

With a little bit of a whiney tone in my voice, I said, "Well...it's been just a little tough. This is all such a big adjustment. I don't know if shining shoes is right for me. When I mentioned it to the woman of my dreams, she broke up with me on the spot."

Jim rolled his eyes, looked at me, and asked sarcastically, "Do you have any cheese to go with that whine? Did you expect it to be easy? If it's easy, it ain't worth it. I know the situation with Abby isn't what you expected. Things will work out. Give it some time."

After pausing, I replied reluctantly, "OK, I'll trust you. I don't know what I expected. In general, the day has gone well. I stopped at two dealerships and the salesmen were all open to letting me shine their shoes. I'm surprised at how nice everyone has been and the money I've made."

"Have you learned anything?"

"Oh, yeah."

"If you're learning, you're growing. If you're growing, you're moving in the right direction."

"I guess you're right. I've met some cool people today. But, I think you already knew that."

With a smile on his face, Jim said, "But, you needed to tell me anyway. You need to experience the excitement."

"I am pretty excited. And it surprises me."

"Good. You never thought you'd ever be excited about shining shoes for other people…did you?"

"No, I didn't. But, actually I am. How 'bout that."

"Yeah. How about that? That's a good sign."

"What's a good sign?" I asked.

"Excitement…excitement usually means it's getting to you. It's affecting you. When it starts affecting you, then you can really start affecting other people."

"Yeah. I guess you're right."

Jim smiled, "I usually am." After a brief pause, he continued. "Always keep this in mind. ***It's not what you are that holds you back…it's what you think you are not.***"

He then wiped his face off with a towel and said, "I'm finished with my workout. I'll see you later." He turned and walked away, as I stood in the same spot thinking about our conversation.

After a moment, I thought to myself, *Yeah, Jim. I'll see you later.*

A couple of minutes after that, another thought entered my mind, *I'd better go see Bob Jennings and work out something if I'm going to shine shoes here at the Y.*

As I walked down the steps to the locker room, Bob was coming up. We met on the landing.

I said, "Hi, Bob. I'm Gary Neal. I hope you remember us talking about me possibly shining shoes here at the Y."

"Oh, yes. I remember quite well! I'd be delighted to work that out for you. Let's look at the area where the former shoeshine guy had been set up."

I followed him down the rest of the steps, where he showed me an open space around a corner. There was a small closet right behind it.

"Here's a nice spot. You'll have a storage closet to keep your things."

Looking at the space, I noticed it was right beside the entrance to the men's locker room, which was exactly where I had envisioned earlier. I knew I could catch all the guys going in to change clothes when they first arrived, and that would be a great time for them to leave me their shoes so I could shine them while they were working out.

I said, "Bob, this is awesome. Thanks so much for your cooperation and support." At that, I gave him a big smile and said, "Well, I guess I'm your new shoeshine guy! I'll see you tomorrow, and thanks again for everything."

He shook my hand and said, "See ya tomorrow."

CHAPTER TWENTY-THREE

The next day, I was set up and shining shoes near the base of the steps at the spot the director had suggested. I had one of the pictures of Abby taped to a cabinet next to me, so I could look at it throughout the day. On my boom box, a CD was playing a song named, *Snap Your Fingers.* That put me in a good mood. I began to hum, as I continued shining shoes. Things were beginning to work out.

About that time, a tall, sharply dressed athletic man in his thirties walked up and smiled.

I turned down the volume of my music so we could speak.

He introduced himself, "I'm Brandon Murphy. How are you doing?"

"Doing great! I'm Gary Neal. Glad to meet you," I said.

"So, we have a shoeshine guy now? How long have you been working here?"

"Just started today."

"I thought you were new. I haven't been here in a couple of weeks."

"Traveling?"

"No. A big case. I'm a lawyer. Have you been shining shoes very long?"

"Yes and no."

"What does that mean?"

"I've had years of practice shining my own shoes. But, I just started doing it for others yesterday."

"You don't dress like any shoeshine guy I've ever seen. I like the hat you're wearing."

"Thanks."

"Do you just work here?"

"No. I'll be here early in the morning, then I'll go out to visit various car dealerships. Later in the day, I'll try to get back here by four o'clock or so."

"That means you could come to our office. We have about twenty in our firm. I'm sure they would all love to have their shoes done. Could you come by once a week in the middle of the day?"

"Yeah, sure."

I reached over to get one of my business cards to give Brandon. When I handed it to him, he handed one of his to me. "Here's my card. Just give me a call, and we'll work out the details. If I leave my shoes with you now, can I pick them up in about an hour?"

"Absolutely."

"OK. I'll see you later. Nice meeting you. I'm on my way to the locker room to change for a quick workout."

Brandon took off both shoes, left them with me, picked up his gym bag and started to leave.

I said, "Thanks. I appreciate it, and I'll give you a call at your office. I can come by this week to shine everyone's shoes."

After he left, I turned the volume back up on my boom box and continued polishing the shoes in front of me.

CHAPTER TWENTY-FOUR

That night, Brandon was driving his car and speaking into a recorder.

He said, "Tell Rebecca to get Markell Robinson's deposition. Call Claudia at the D.A.'s office to get the files on Walt Steinfield. Call Lisa Johnson about lunch. Send Alice a nice bouquet of flowers."

Putting the recorder on his seat, he thought, *I need to get something to drink.*

He pulled into a convenience store parking lot, got out of the car, and walked inside.

A young, male clerk was standing behind the counter.

"What's up?" Brandon asked.

"Not much. How're you doing?"

"Fine. I'm just here to get a soda from your drink machine."

Brandon walked over to the machine, took a cup and filled it with ice. Then, he added a diet drink to it. He went up to the man at the cash register to pay. While the clerk was ringing up the sale, two rough looking guys entered the front door of the store with handguns. One was a short male with black hair slicked back on his head. He wore a white T shirt that exposed a large tattoo on his right forearm. The other man was taller, hadn't shaved in days, and was visibly nervous.

The first guy bellowed in a loud voice, "Everybody... freeze!" Then, he turned to the clerk and demanded, "Hand over all the money in the cash register and don't be stupid." He shouted, "HURRY UP!"

The young clerk opened the cash register. With shaking hands, he took out all the bills and handed them to the robber. The thief put the money in a bag he pulled from his pocket and quickly headed toward the door. He opened it, looked around and left in a hurry. He then came back, reopened the door, and poked his head inside.

"Come on, Ray. Let's go!!"

By that time, Ray had approached Brandon and placed his gun barrel to Brandon's forehead. The hand holding the gun was shaking, and it was obvious Ray was out of control.

"Mr. Murphy. Long time...no see. Didn't think you'd see me again, did ya? And, not like this."

Brandon was instantly terrified. He remembered the man from his past. He was so nervous the drink slipped from his hand and hit the floor.

"I've been out for a week." Gritting his teeth and raising his voice, he said, "A week."

"Ray, I did the best I could. I got you the shortest time they would allow."

With anger in his voice, Ray said, "It wasn't short enough. The cops screwed up and you knew it. You should've gotten me off. I guess you screwed up, too."

Brandon stared at the gun with its barrel of cold steel pushed against his head. With a shaky voice, he pleaded, "Please. Don't, Ray. Please."

Ray pulled the trigger. There was a dead silence as both men realized what had happened. The gun had jammed. It did not go off. Brandon jumped backward with his eyes closed tightly. Ray pulled the gun away.

"Well, you jerk, looks like this is your lucky night."

His partner standing at the door shouted, "Ray, let's go." In a louder voice, he screamed, "Let's get the hell out of here! Right now!"

Ray backed away slowly, but not before first staring intensely at Brandon. After meeting his accomplice at the door, they both ran across the parking lot. They stopped briefly, looked around to see if any cars were coming, then began to run down the street and disappeared into the darkness.

The clerk picked up his phone and called the police to report the robbery and assault.

Brandon sat down on a case of sodas stacked near the counter, still in shock. He looked up and noticed an African-American man. He was dressed immaculately...with very shiny shoes, walking toward him.

"Where did you come from?" Brandon asked.

"I was standing in the back of the store and observed the whole thing. That must have been frightening to have a loaded gun pointed at your head. My name is Virgil. Do you think you're going to be alright?"

Brandon glanced down at Virgil's highly polished shoes and looked up.

"Yeah. I think so. My name is Brandon Murphy. I'm glad to meet you. It may take a while to settle my nerves, and that's an understatement. I'm extremely shaken-up right now."

Virgil handed Brandon a diet soda and said, "I saw where you dropped your drink. Here, I grabbed you another one. It's on me."

Brandon took the drink and Virgil sat down on another case of sodas beside him.

"Thanks. Did you see everything that happened?"

"Yes," Virgil said.

"He pulled the trigger and the gun didn't go off. Can you believe that?"

"Yes, I can. It wasn't your time."

"Ya think so?" Brandon asked shakily.

"I know so. You'll find out pretty soon what I'm talking about...after everything returns to normal."

Virgil reached over and patted Brandon on the knee and then got up. He extended his hand to Brandon, and they both shook. A siren blared in the distance, then shortly afterward a police car stopped outside.

"Come on." Virgil said. "The police are here. Let's go talk with them about what happened."

Virgil tugged Brandon to his feet, and together they walked to the front door to meet the two officers who had just gotten out of their patrol car and were coming toward them.

The first policeman walked directly to the front counter

to talk with the clerk. The second policeman approached Brandon and Virgil with a notepad in his hand.

He asked Brandon, "Were you here when the robbery occurred?"

"Yes, sir," Brandon replied.

"Did you get a good look at the men? Do you think you could identify them?"

"Yes."

"Could you pick them out in a line-up?"

"Actually, I know one of them personally."

"How so?"

"I'm a lawyer. I defended him last year. He was ticked off about his sentence. Just a few moments ago, he put his gun to my forehead and pulled the trigger. It jammed."

"Whoa...you OK?"

"Yeah...I think so."

"What's his name?"

"Ray Glass."

The policeman wrote the name on his notepad and then asked Brandon, "Can you come down to the station and make a statement?"

"Yes. Can I follow you in my car?"

"Sure. But first, come sit in my squad car. We may have a few more questions before going to the station."

"No problem. That'll be fine with me."

The officer then turned to face Virgil.

"Did you see anything?"

"I saw everything," Virgil responded.

"Would you also be willing to come down to the station and make a statement?"

"Be happy to."

"Thank you, sir. Please, go have a seat in our car, too. We shouldn't be much longer.

The other policeman asked the young clerk a series of questions similar to those that had been asked to Brandon and Virgil. The clerk gave him all the information necessary and said, "I'll be glad to go to the station and make a statement, but I'll need to wait until I get off from work."

"That will be fine," said the policeman. "Come by in a few hours, and we'll fill out all the necessary paperwork. Your complete cooperation will be appreciated. In the meantime, we'll get all the information we can from the two other gentlemen who were here during the incident."

CHAPTER TWENTY-FIVE

I laid out all my stuff near the bottom of the steps at the Y the next morning. As I positioned my shoeshine box for the start of business, I couldn't help but see Abby's photo taped to the inside while getting my supplies out of it. I noticed that photo, even though another one was also taped to the cabinet nearby. Looking at the pictures and listening to my boom box's CD player, one of Frank Sinatra's hits blared out, welling up sadness inside me. The song was *I've Got You Under My Skin*. I turned down the volume slightly. The words seemed to resonate within my soul.

From across the room, I noticed a man approaching. He walked straight up to me and introduced himself. I turned the volume on the CD player down even more, so we could talk and hear each other clearly.

"My name is John Jones. I work with Brandon Murphy. You met Brandon yesterday."

"Yes, a very nice man. I did his shoes and enjoyed talking with him."

"He's not going to be able to stop by for a couple of weeks. He wanted me to ask you if you could come by our law office this Thursday around ten o'clock in the morning. A few of us, including Brandon, want our shoes done."

"This Thursday? Sure. Be glad to," I said.

"You know where we're located, don't you?"

"Yeah. Brandon gave me the information."

John wanted to make sure I had the correct location and all the information, so he kept talking.

"Near the Union Station building downtown."

"Yep, that's what Brandon told me."

Then he added, "We're across the street…the brown brick building. Fifth floor…suite 515. Just let the receptionist know who you are. She'll call Brandon to come out front and meet you at her desk."

"Very good. See you Thursday."

After John walked away, I reached down and turned the volume back up on the player.

I thought to myself, *That's cool. I'll be able to meet a bunch of Brandon's lawyer friends and shine a lot of shoes on Thursday.*

CHAPTER TWENTY-SIX

The next few days passed quickly. It was Thursday morning before I knew it. Entering Brandon's lobby with my shoeshine box in hand, I walked up to the receptionist and smiled.

She asked, "May I help you?"

"I'm Gary Neal. Brandon Murphy is expecting me."

Picking up the phone and dialing his number, she smiled at me, and gestured it would only be a second.

She said into the phone when Brandon answered, "There's a Gary Neal to see you in the lobby. He said you were expecting him this morning. OK, I'll tell him."

"Brandon will be right with you. Just have a seat."

"Thank you."

I walked across the room admiring the artwork on the walls. It was an impressive place. I took a seat on a nice upholstered sofa and briefly began watching a TV that was broadcasting a local news program.

A couple of minutes later, Brandon entered the room and

walked up to me. "Hey, Gary, good to see you. Thanks for coming," he said, as he shook my hand.

"Good to see you."

"Let's go to my office." We walked together down a hallway, as he started talking. "I want you to do my shoes first. Then, I'll take you to the conference room where the rest of the shoes are already laid out. The other lawyers are excited about getting their shoes done and have brought in a number of extra pairs for you."

"That's great. I'm looking forward to getting started."

As we entered Brandon's plush office, he sat down behind his desk and said, "Pull up one of those chairs. That way we can talk while you're working."

"Sure."

I sat down and began to get my stuff out of the box. I noticed again Abby's picture taped to the inside. Brandon lifted his first foot and put his shoe on the top of the box. I began to shine as we talked.

"You been staying busy?" Brandon asked.

"Yeah. Pretty much."

I pulled out a small, clear spray bottle of water, which had been labeled *Secret Sauce* with a sharpie pen and set it to the side of my box. I could tell Brandon was curious. It was regularly used after adding the wax polish and during the buffing process so the end result was a very high shine.

"Secret sauce?" He asked, while smiling. "What's in it?"

I smiled and looked up. Then, I looked back down without answering.

"Come on. You can tell me."

I said, "Let me ask you a question. Did Colonel Sanders give away the secret recipe for his chicken?"

Brandon laughed, because he knew what was coming. "No. I guess he didn't."

"There you go," I replied with a smile.

"So...I guess you answered that question. Are you doing a lot of shoes at the Y?"

"It's picking up."

"It does seem like you're having fun with it. I've noticed you play a lot of Sinatra's hits while you work."

"YES, I DO." I replied in a sing-song voice and continued to smile.

"Are you a big fan of Frank's?"

"Oh, yeah. He was more than just a great singer. He had class. Sang with class, dressed with class, and lived life with class. He was all class. That's why I dress the way I do...even the hat. I try to do what I do with class. I use what I call the 'Frank philosophy'...Fun with a capital F. And I try to do everything naturally 'Kool,' like Frank."

With a laugh, Brandon responded, "Yeah. I get it. That's Kool...with a capital K. What did you do before you started shining shoes?"

"I was always in the car business."

"Really? What made you decide to change and get into this line of work?"

"Needed to make some big changes in my life," I said.

"You think you made the right choice?"

"At first, I wasn't sure. But each day I'm seeing more and more that I did make the right decision."

"I guess I'm kind'a in the same spot myself," he said.

"What do you mean?"

Brandon answered by saying, "A few days ago I was at a convenience store when two guys robbed it at gunpoint. One of the robbers, before he left, stuck the barrel of his pistol to my forehead and pulled the trigger. The gun jammed. It was freaking unbelievable. I even knew the guy."

"What? You knew the guy??"

"Yeah. I defended him last year. He wasn't happy with the sentence he received, which led to his having to spend time in jail. He recognized me as he was about to leave the store and decided to kill me. I've never been so scared in my life."

"Wow."

"The guy waited for what seemed to be forever before he pulled the trigger. Actually, it was only five to ten seconds. I didn't think he would do it, but he did," Brandon said.

"Did he say anything to you?"

"Yes. Afterwards, he said it must be my lucky night."

"Sounds like it was."

"Do you believe in luck?" Brandon asked.

I responded, "Brandon, I've gotten to the point lately that I believe in something much bigger that has nothing to do with luck. A special friend has helped me arrive at this place in my life. I'm now convinced that everyone carries a gift within themselves. That gift can affect people…touch people, in a unique way. I've learned just recently that when I share my gift, it opens doors and offers me unique opportunities to go to places where I can help others. Obviously, you have a gift, also. You've got to ask yourself if your gift is just helping you, or is it helping other people…making a difference. Are people better off…even just a little…when you share your gift?"

"Wow. I've never thought about that before. You've explained it so clearly. Do you really think I have a gift…like you're talking about?" Brandon asked.

"Maybe your gift is your knowledge of the law. Maybe there's something different you can do with all you've learned in that area. It could be that you can start using that special gift to help people in new ways where they can't help themselves."

"I do know this. After what happened to me in the convenience store, I can't go back into the courtroom again and put crooks back on the street. The guy who put the pistol to my forehead, I knew he was guilty at the time I defended him. By using some mistakes the detectives had made, I got him a lesser sentence. I'm not going to do that again."

"Good for you," I said.

"You know, I've never told anyone this before…ever. I really hate being a lawyer. I only did it for my mom. When I was a kid, she had a car accident. She was driving us home from school. A kid ran in front of her, coming out from between two parked cars, chasing a ball that went into the street. She swerved to miss him and hit an elderly lady sitting on a bench waiting for the bus. Mom had to pay everything she had for the lady's hospital bills. We couldn't afford a lawyer. The old lady saw the kid run in front of the car, but she lied in court. She claimed Mom just ran off the road and hit her for no reason. There was no one to help Mom legally, and we lost our house. We moved in with her sister in a little apartment for two years until she met my stepdad. She always told me afterwards, 'Poor people need lawyers too.' I was pushed by her to go to college and then to law school."

I asked Brandon an important question in response to his long explanation, as I started working on his second shoe. "What do you really want to do?"

Brandon laughed and looked directly at me. At first, he was reluctant to speak, but answered. "Gary, I've always wanted to be a detective. I feel that people who are victims need real help. They need somebody watching out for them."

"You can do that," I said.

"How so?"

"You already know the law. You regularly work with detectives. You're aware of how to catch their mistakes. That's your gift. Knowing what you know, you can keep the bad guys off the street. You can help the victims. You can become a detective."

"You know what, Gary, I think you're right. I can do just that. Yes, I can."

Getting up after having finished his second shoe, I asked, "So…what are you going to do?"

"First, I'm gonna make some phone calls." Laughing to himself, he said, "I've got some serious investigating to do about my future on how to become a detective."

"Good for you."

Brandon looked down at his shoes. "Wow! Thanks!"

"My pleasure."

"How much do I owe you?"

"Five dollars."

"Here's twenty-five dollars. I feel it's a bargain. You've given me some very helpful advice while doing my shoes. I appreciate it and hope to soon take advantage of what you've suggested." Looking down at his shoes once more, he added, "Man, when I shine my shoes, I can't get them to look this good. What's your secret? And I'm not talking about the sauce."

"Well, when you shine your shoes, it's because you have to. When I shine shoes, it's because I love to. Maybe that's the real secret," I said.

Brandon got up and walked toward his door, as I put everything back in my shoeshine box and followed him.

"Yeah, I think you're right. Come on. I'll show you where the conference room is located. There's a bunch of shoes waiting for you there."

After directing me to the room, he reached out and shook my hand. With a big, happy smile, he said, "Hey, man. Thanks...with all my heart." With that, he gave me a big hug.

"You are definitely welcome. I now need to get started on all these shoes. Look at all the fun I'm going to have," I said.

CHAPTER TWENTY-SEVEN

Two months later, there were eight people present in the police squad room. Brandon walked in with the chief of detectives. The chief began talking to all the detectives he had in front of him.

"Guys, I want you to meet Brandon Murphy. Some of you may recognize him. He used to work at the law firm of Holcomb, Willis, and Woodward. He just passed his detective exam. Brandon will be going through a detailed training orientation, working and observing each of you for the next six months. He's in a special program, so he'll be asking you guys a lot of questions while out in the field. After a couple of months, he'll have a partner assigned and will become a full-fledged detective. Let's welcome him aboard and make him feel like one of the team. I'll let you each introduce yourselves to him."

With that said, the chief patted him on the shoulder, then

added, "Welcome to our unit. I want to talk with you again before you leave."

The chief left the room and each detective walked up to Brandon and introduced himself before most of them went on to other things down the hall.

Only detective Pete Tiller, detective Philip Martin, and Brandon stayed behind. Martin closed the door.

"Murphy, right?" Martin said.

"Right."

"So…how does a shyster lawyer putting thugs back on the street become a detective?" He asked this with a smirk on his face.

"Excuse me?"

"Why the switch in jobs? Why become a detective after being a defender of the guilty?"

"Let's just say I had a change of heart."

With that, Martin angrily pointed at Brandon and walked up close to his face to make an impression.

"Don't play me, Murphy. I sat in the box during two of your cases. Both times you tried to make me look like I should have been on trial. You made me look like a total screw-up… just for doing my job."

Brandon said back to him, "At the time, I was just doing my job. Maybe I'm too late, but I'm sorry for that now. I've decided that now I want to keep the thugs off the streets. That's why I've made the switch. You don't have to believe me, but it's the truth."

Detective Tiller asked, "So, why the change of heart?"

"A couple of months ago, I was present during an armed

robbery at a convenience store. I knew one of the robbers, and he knew me. He was a guy I had previously represented in court, and one I had negotiated a reduced sentence for, from five years to six months. He felt I should have kept him out of jail completely, so he put a gun to my forehead. He pulled the trigger. The gun jammed. I knew right then I wasn't ever going back into a court room...at least not as a lawyer."

Martin responded, "No wonder you changed your mind. One of your street thugs almost killed you. You got a little taste of how we feel. So now you're one of us? Well...let me tell you something counselor...the rules here are different. Welcome to the Sewage Department. Life will never be the same. I'm the senior detective. Been here the longest, and I'm now your daddy. Don't think for a second we're gonna cut you any slack. We don't trust you, and I'm not sure I believe that story about why you're here. We don't like this new program where they recruit from the outside for detectives. All of us got our shields the hard way...out there on the streets."

"Look guys, I'm not expecting any slack. But I am gonna do my job. And I'm going to do it well...by the book."

"By the book...huh?" asked Detective Martin.

With that said, he walked across the room to a closet near the far corner. He unlocked the door, bent down to work the combination, and opened a small safe. There was a book inside that he lifted out, brought back across the room, and set on top of his desk.

"Good. I'm glad you said that. That's the way we do things here. By the book...this book."

"What's that?" Brandon asked.

Picking up the book and showing it to Brandon, Martin said, "Counselor, this is the *Book of Knowledge*. You may know the law, but I know the streets. And on the streets, I'm the law."

Martin then began to flip through the pages.

"This book contains a ton of street-smart information. That type of information contains a lot of power. With your knowledge of the law, you can rock their world using what's in this book."

Brandon asked, "What do you mean?"

"Murphy, we both know there's a lot of scum out there. Catching them is one thing, keeping them in the slammer is another thing altogether. You know how that goes. But, here's how it works on this side. We can keep roping them in, but the system just keeps untying them, and they go back out. Once we get them, we log them in this book. We keep tabs on them. They then help us, and we help them in return. They don't help...they pay...one way or the other."

"They pay how?"

"They either pay with money or with information. They know and see things we don't. We know things they don't. When we need help, we cash in on their eyes and ears. If they don't pay us with information, they pay us with money. One way or the other, they pay. Our policy is, once they're brought in and then go back, we own them. To be able to stay out of here, they pay. That's why we get valuable evidence when we need it."

"What if they're not really guilty of a crime when they're originally brought in?" Brandon asked.

"Come on, Murphy. You're smarter than that. We're the ones who decide if they're guilty or not. Not the system."

"So, even if someone is not guilty of something, and they owe you and can't pay with information or money, you fabricate evidence from others to get a case against them."

"You're gettin' smarter already. See how nicely it all works?"

Brandon asked, "That's why your arrest and conviction rate is so high…right?"

Detective Martin shrugged his shoulders and cracked a big smile. Brandon began to walk around the room, as he thought about what he had learned.

"Man, what you're doing is not right. That means you put people away who aren't guilty. And, some of the guilty ones are still out there. For them to be able to stay out there, they pay…is that how it works?"

Detective Martin then turned around to face Detective Tiller, who'd been standing quietly to one side of the room.

Martin said to Tiller, "He's catching on quick."

To Brandon, he said with a smile, "With what you know about the law, you'll be a great asset. You know what I mean?"

"Are you guys for real? You can't be serious about this."

"Look at me," Martin said, with an intense scowl. "You bet your life we're serious."

Walking over and pressing a finger into Brandon's chest to make his point, he said, "Now don't even think about sharing this conversation with anybody else…because…it never happened."

He then walked over and sat on the corner of his desk and continued to talk.

"You've heard about those detectives they caught taking bribes...those who were squeezing other thugs. How do you think they were found out? They were taken out because they were beginning to be a problem. They couldn't keep their mouths shut. That led to them going to jail. So, if you're as smart as I think you are, you'll know what to do."

Martin then stood and walked across the room with the book in his hand. He looked over at Tiller, who had been standing quietly, listening to everything that had been said.

Martin said to Brandon with sarcasm in his voice, "Oh... by the way...welcome aboard."

He took the book back to the closet and placed it inside the safe. The door was closed, and the combination lock was spun. He locked the closet using his key and then put it in his right front pocket.

With that, Martin and Tiller left the room. Brandon stood and stared into space. He was definitely rattled. After a short moment, he regained his senses, picked up his study manual and left the room. He walked down the hall and found an empty room, so he could sit quietly and start looking through the guide he needed to master.

CHAPTER TWENTY-EIGHT

Steps were heard coming down the hall, and a figure entered the doorway. It was the chief, and he walked over to the desk where Brandon was sitting.

"Why don't you call it a night?"

"I'm gonna look through this manual a little longer before I go. There's a lot to digest." Brandon said, as he leaned back in the chair.

Patting Brandon on the shoulder, the chief said, "It's great to have you as part of our team. If you need any help, don't hesitate to ask. OK?"

"OK. Thanks."

"Good night," the chief said.

"Good night."

The chief then left the room and his footsteps echoed on the tile floor as he went down the hallway.

Looking up, Brandon began to think about all that had

just happened. He knew what he'd heard from Martin wasn't right, and was sure the chief didn't know anything about it. He felt positive the chief would be furious if he had any idea about the book, and how it was used. What he had to decide was what to do next.

Brandon got up, went down the hallway to the coffee area, found a cup, and poured himself some coffee. While drinking, he walked around the room deep in thought. He was very disturbed at what he'd been told the book contained, and how it was affecting innocent people. After finishing his cup, he returned to the office where he'd been sitting.

As he walked into the room, he noticed something different. Lying on top of his manual in the middle of the desk was a black book. At first glance, it looked similar to the one Martin had shown him earlier. When he got closer, he stopped and looked around. He'd passed no one in the hallway, and there was no one anywhere around.

"Who's here?" he asked out loud.

There was no reply. Brandon walked out of the office and down the hall a short distance to make sure no one was nearby. He then went back inside the office, sat down, and began to stare at the book that had appeared out of nowhere. Picking it up, he started to thumb through the pages. For a full thirty minutes, he studied its contents...one page at a time.

Geeeeez...Holy Crap, he thought over and over, as he read what was written inside.

Finally, closing the book, he got out of his chair and began to walk around the room in order to take time to think more deeply. He paced back and forth, rubbing his neck. Walking over to the desk, he put both hands on it, leaned forward and stared at the book.

In his mind, he could remember the words spoken earlier by Detective Martin. *If you're as smart as I think you are, you'll know what to do.*

The location of the chief's office down the hall had been pointed out to him. Dropping his head and looking at the floor, he knew what he had to do. With the book in hand, he slowly walked toward the chief's office. Stopping at the door, he paused for a moment. Testing the knob, he realized it had not been locked. He went over to the chief's desk and laid the book in the center of his chair, so it couldn't be missed the next morning.

Walking out, he closed the door, and returned to the office where he'd been studying. He put on his coat and picked up the manual. Turning off the desk lamp, he stood silently for a few more seconds, and then left to go home.

CHAPTER TWENTY-NINE

Brandon was still looking through the procedure manual while sitting at his new desk around lunch time the next day.

In walked the chief, who came up to him and asked in a very serious voice, "Brandon, can you come down to my office right now?"

He quickly got out of his chair and followed the chief to his office. The older man let him go in first and went over to sit down behind his desk.

"Have a seat, Brandon."

He sat down in a chair already in place.

The chief glanced at the top of his desk. Rubbing his hands over his mouth, he reached into a drawer and pulled out the book.

Lifting it up, he asked, "Do you know anything about this?"

Brandon swallowed hard and replied, "What do you mean, sir?"

"My meaning should be clear. Look, this morning, I found this book lying in my chair when I came in. It wasn't there when I left last night. When I got out of here, you were the only one still around. Oddly enough, I forgot to lock my door."

Leaning forward in his chair with both of his hands on his desk, he continued. "Be straight with me. Did you put it there?"

Brandon looked away, thought for a moment, cleared his throat, and then looked back at the chief.

"I did, chief. I put it there before I left last night."

"How did you get hold of it?"

"After you left, I went to get some coffee. I wasn't gone over ten minutes. When I came back to my desk, it was lying on top of my new procedure manual right in front of me."

"Did you read any of it?"

"Yes sir, and I realize what it is."

"Look. I know you're brand new. Actually, you're not even official yet. You've just opened a can…a whole barrel… of worms. And, there's no telling how deep this all goes." The chief paused to compose himself and then continued. "I've known we've had a bad apple in the department, but we could never figure out who it was. Now, I find out through this book, there was more than one. We've been investigating internally for over two years. Only four people, including me and the commissioner, knew about the investigation. I suspect there are many in jail right now who are totally innocent, including two detectives and three uniformed cops." After a slight hesitation, he went on. "This book tells the complete story of what was going on. I've been reading through it all morning. You've really stirred up a deep pot of corruption by giving me this."

Just as that was said, Martin and Tiller walked by the chief's open door, escorted by a uniformed policeman. They were both wearing handcuffs. As they passed, they glared in at the new man with a *look to kill* stare.

The chief turned to Brandon and asked, "Are you sure you don't know how it suddenly appeared on your desk?"

"No sir. It was just there, on the top of the desk, when I returned from getting my coffee last night."

"Well, I'll tell you what. You've really got to watch yourself, now. I'm not sure who you can trust and who you can't. I thought I did...but now I'm not sure at all. I do know this though, Brandon. You can trust me...totally. Do you believe that?"

"Yes sir, I do."

"Good. You've got some soul searching to do now. We should probably transfer you to get you out of this building. It's going to be rough if they suspect you for this shake-up. Trust is a hard wall to climb. You've gotta ask yourself, "Do you really want to do this job?""

After a short hesitation, Brandon responded, "Yes, I do." Then, with a slight shake of his head, he repeated, "I do, definitely...I have to."

"OK."

The chief rose from his chair, walked around his desk toward Brandon, and shook his hand.

"Thanks, chief."

"Go back down to your office, and I'll let you know where to report. We'll move you out of here for your own safety. You'll still be doing detective work."

Brandon said, "I understand." He then left the room.

The chief sat back down. He rubbed one hand over his face and started on some paperwork. While working, he thought about how proud he was of Brandon's actions. His plans were to definitely make sure Brandon was protected. There wasn't any doubt in his mind this new man was on his way to a long and successful career as one of his top detectives.

Chapter Thirty

I stopped by Dimples Diner and parked my truck in the front. After getting out, I followed my normal routine and bought a newspaper from the coin-operated metal box outside. Going through the door, I noticed my regular booth was still open and took a seat near the cash register. A major headline on the newspaper's front page couldn't be ignored. It read POLICE CORRUPTION EXPOSED in bold print.

The waitress poured me a cup of coffee out of habit, so I thanked her. She put a menu on the table, but I avoided looking at it, because I already knew what I wanted. She quickly walked away, giving me some time anyway, as I became interested in the article.

It read, "Two innocent men who were put into prison on false evidence are being released today. The released men are assistant detectives who had knowledge of a city-wide ring of corruption. They have helped officers identify many of those guilty of local robberies and thefts."

Across the room, I could hear a group of men laughing. Looking at them closely, I noticed one was Jim, and there were four others with him. They were all standing, as if they were about to leave. I stood and walked across the room.

When they saw me coming, the four of them walked right past, but not before each one either called me by name and said, "Hello, Gary," or just acknowledged with a quick nod that they knew me.

I recognized the last one as Virgil, and was puzzled that he passed me so quickly.

Jim took a seat and I sat down across from him. Then he asked, "Hey, what's up?"

"Just getting some breakfast. Who are those guys? I've seen one of them before," I said.

"Some friends of mine."

"How did they all know my name? Did you tell them?"

"Yep."

"Have you seen this morning's paper?" I asked.

"Why?"

"It says that an internal investigation at the local police department uncovered a major corruption ring in the detective's division. It was all due to an unspecified internal source."

"You don't say?"

The waitress then stopped by our table. She said to me in a nice voice, "Sweetie, you left your coffee and newspaper at the other table. You must have something important on your mind. Are you going to have breakfast over here or at your usual booth?"

"I'll just eat over here. I'm Gary, what's your name?"

"April…just April. I see you every time you come in. Sorry I've not introduced myself before now."

"Hello, April. This is my friend…"

April interrupted and said, "I know Jim."

Looking at Jim, I asked, "So…the two of you already know each other?"

At that, Jim didn't reply, but looked at me as if I should know the answer to the question.

"What can I get you this morning?" April asked.

"I'll have my usual. Two eggs over easy, sausage, and toast."

She walked toward the kitchen to place my order, and I looked at Jim.

I said, "Didn't know you came here for breakfast."

"This isn't the only place we meet."

"Meet? Meet for what?"

"To talk about our assignments. Make preparations. Give each other advice. That kind of stuff."

I asked, "Talk about your assignments? Are all those guys like you?"

"Yep."

"Wait a minute…one of those guys was the first pair of shoes I shined my first day. I shined them across town at a new restaurant near the interstate." I stopped and thought for a few seconds before continuing. "You sent him, didn't you? Wait a minute…I went there that particular morning on a fluke. How did you know when to send him…where to send him?"

Jim just looked at me with his 'you're kidding' face.

I then began to put it all together. "So, what's his name?" I asked.

"Virgil," Jim said.

"What's his last name?"

"He doesn't have one."

"What?"

"Neither do I," Jim said.

CHAPTER THIRTY-ONE

About that time, the waitress brought my meal, along with my coffee and newspaper, and set it all down in front of me. Apparently, Jim had already eaten.

I said to her, "Thank you. This looks very nice."

She replied, "Glad to hear, Honey. Enjoy it." She then walked over to a table at the other side of the room to help another one of her customers.

I continued with my questioning, as I began to eat. "You really don't have a last name?"

"Don't need one."

"Why?"

"Too complicated."

"Too complicated?" I asked. "How complicated can a last name be?"

"If I told you my real name, it would just confuse you. So, it's best to keep things simple. That way you don't focus too much on us. We're not here for the attention or praise. We're here for you, or whoever we're assigned to. You see, names are not really important. They're just something you can use or refer to for convenience."

I said, "I've got a question, but I'm kind of afraid of what the answer might be." After a short pause, I asked anyway. "Do you know my dad?"

"Why do you ask?"

"When I told him about meeting you, he revealed to me that he'd had a similar encounter in the past. He told me he'd never said anything about it to anyone. A special person had saved his life when he was young, and he'd been told it was for a reason. He described that person as looking very much like you. He said his name was also Jim. So…was that you? Were you that person, too?"

"Does it matter?"

"I want to know. Were you or not…?" I asked.

"Don't make things too complicated. Learn to let things happen. You worry about everything. Do what you're supposed to, and let the rest take care of itself. You'll be a lot happier and life will be so much easier. Trust me. Don't worry about what's happened before. You need to focus on now. What you do now affects what happens later. If it has already happened, there's nothing you can do about it."

I took a deep breath, realizing he was right, and simply asked, "Have you always been around?"

"Yep."

"Since I was a kid?"

"Yep." After a brief pause, Jim asked me, "Remember

when you were young, and your dad took the training wheels off your bike?"

"Yeah, I do."

"Remember going down that big hill and you couldn't get the brakes to work? When you lost control of your bike and landed on a big pile of leaves right before you got to the bottom...where the cars were whizzing by?"

"You did that?"

With a blank stare, Jim lowered his head and then looked back up at me.

"Darn," I said. "That was the only place around there with leaves piled up. You probably saved my life that day."

He then opened up both hands, made a gesture, and said, "There you go."

"What else did you do?"

Jim thought for a moment and began to laugh.

"I shouldn't brag, but remember when you were sixteen, and you hadn't had your license very long? You had a flat tire, and you would've missed your curfew. Lucky for you that guy came by in a truck. Changed your tire pretty fast...didn't I?"

Leaning forward in amazement, I asked, "That was you?"

"Yep."

"But...he...you...had a beard...and a lot more hair."

"Looked like a hippie, didn't I?"

"Yes, you did."

"Had to keep up with the times," Jim said, with a laugh.

"So, I've met you before?"

With that question, Jim looked at me strangely.

Reflecting backward, I began to think about many different

things that had occurred in my life, which hadn't made sense at the time.

"This is weird," I said. While leaning back in my seat, I added, "Whoa…it's all absolutely unbelievable."

"Yeah, I know."

"So…those other guys…they do for others what you do for me?"

"Pretty much."

"I've got a friend named Brandon. He was in a nearby convenience store during a robbery."

"You mean when the gun didn't go off?"

"You know about that?"

"Yep. One of those other guys in here earlier takes care of Brandon."

"Which one?"

"Virgil…your first shoeshine. Do you remember why he got his shoes shined?"

After thinking about it, I said, "No."

"Remember when he said he had an important meeting that night?"

"Yeah. I do remember him telling me that."

"He was meeting Brandon at the convenience store during the robbery."

"Wow!" I said, in an astonished voice.

"His shoes were the first thing about him Brandon saw," Jim said.

"So, Virgil caused the gun to jam? Right?"

Jim made no comment but just kept looking at me as things continued to fall in place.

Glancing down at my watch, I noticed the time had slipped away. I got out of my seat, took my keys from my pocket and said, "Dang, I gotta go."

"I gotta go, too. You've got to get to work."

I said, "Yes, I do."

"You're headed to Brentwood."

Taken off guard by his statement, I asked, "How did you know?"

Jim almost laughed and then went on to say, "Today is going to be a good day."

"I hope so," I replied.

"It will. Trust me. You won't see it for a while, but today is going to be a big day for you. So, get going."

"Yeah, I guess I'd better."

Getting up from the table, I left the newspaper and a twenty dollar bill for the waitress.

To Jim, I said, "See you later."

CHAPTER THIRTY-TWO

Driving my truck to a Cadillac dealership where I knew a few of the salesmen and had shined some shoes five days earlier, I turned up the music on my radio. After parking, I waited in their lot until a song finished before getting out with my shoeshine box and walking inside. I only had about 30 minutes before I had to be at the Y, but thought I could shine at least a few pairs of shoes.

Passing one of the salesmen near the front door, I said, "Hello," before going to the receptionist's desk. I didn't have a chance to greet her before my good friend Chuck Hanes, the sales manager, walked by.

He said, "Hey Gary, you got a minute?"

"Sure."

"Come with me. I have someone special I want you to meet. I want you to shine the boots of a country music legend."

Not knowing what to expect, I followed him into his office. Seated in front of his desk was Billy Stone, the king of country music. I instantly recognized him from seeing his face many times on TV. He was in his sixties, with snow white hair, wire-rimmed glasses, starched jeans, and a fancy cowboy shirt. On his feet were beautiful hand-stitched cowboy boots.

"Billy, I want you to meet a friend of mine. This is the best shoeshine guy there is. Gary, this is Billy Stone."

Billy stood up with a big smile on his face and shook my hand. "Hello there, partner."

"I'm glad to meet you, Mr. Stone. I've seen you on TV many times."

"Billy, while you're waiting for them to appraise your car, Gary's going to shine your boots. How about that?"

Billy looked down at his boots and said, "They definitely would benefit by a good shining. Sure…let me get them off so you can get started."

I placed my shoeshine box on the floor and began to get out the needed items. As I removed the brush and polish, I glanced at the photo of Abby taped to the inside of the box. It reminded me of the last night we were together at the restaurant when I told her she looked so good. For a moment, I was in a trance with that thought and then came back to reality.

Billy said, as he handed me his boots, "I haven't had this done for me in Lord knows how long. I didn't know we had a shoeshine guy with a shop here in the area."

"I don't have a shop," I said. "I'm mobile. I go to where my customers are."

"You mean you could come to my office? I could bring all my boots and shoes, and you would do them all there?"

"Absolutely," I said.

"Well, it looks like I've got my own personal shoeshine

guy. How 'bout that? You don't mind adding me to your list of customers, do you?"

"Not at all. I'd be very glad to do it for you."

"Do you have a card?"

"Yes."

"When you finish, give me your card. I'll have my secretary call you, and we can set up a time for you to come by my office. Will that work for you?"

"That'll work for me."

Chuck then entered the room with some papers in his hand. He sat down at his desk and started writing on them.

"That's what I call a good deal, Chuck. You've hooked me up with a personal shoeshine guy. Now, my boots will look like they're supposed to…all the time." Billy said.

Chuck looked over at me and smiled.

"That's great! Speaking of a good deal, I've got one for you," Chuck said. "When Gary's done, I'll show you some numbers you'll like."

I finished and asked Billy, "Well, sir. What do you think?"

Staring down at his freshly polished boots, he said, "Son, look at that. That's what I'm talking about. Excellent job."

I handed him my business card. "Here's my card. Just give me a call whenever I can help you."

Billy opened his wallet and pulled out one of his cards, which he handed to me. He also began to go through his money to decide how much to pay for the shoeshine.

Chuck quickly said, "Put your money away, Billy. I've got it covered."

"No sir. I'm taking care of this."

Billy then handed me a twenty dollar bill.

"Will that cover my first pair of boots?"

"It will…if you'll autograph it for me," I said.

"Be glad to."

Chuck handed Billy a pen. He autographed the twenty and handed it back to me. "There you go, son."

"Thank you, Mr. Stone."

"That's Billy to you from now on. Next time there'll be a lot of boots…so get ready."

"You got it, Billy."

I put my tools back in the box and stood to leave. "Thanks, Billy, and thanks to you, Chuck."

"See you later, Kemosabe," Chuck said, playfully.

I looked at my watch and saw it was time for me to head to the Y. I left the room and walked to my truck with my box and a big smile.

I said out loud, "I just did Billy Stone's boots. And, I'm going to his office later in the week to do some more work for him. This shoe shining thing isn't so bad after all."

With that, I started my truck and drove away. My next stop would be at the Y where more shoes would be waiting for me.

About two hours later, I was set up in my spot at the bottom of the steps at the Y and was busy shining. There were smiling people walking by. I was feeling good. The boom box was playing one of Sinatra's songs. This one was a big favorite of mine, *Fly Me to the Moon*. I rocked back and forth with the beat.

My cell phone rang, so I reached over and turned down the music.

"Hello, this is Gary. Jackie Sandler? Oh...Billy Stone's assistant. Yes, ma'am. Sure. Wednesday morning? No problem. Nine-thirty sounds good to me. That big building on Music Row? Yes, I know where it's located. I have Billy's card with the address on it. OK. I'll see you Wednesday around nine-thirty. Thanks, Jackie. Tell Billy I'm looking forward to it. Bye."

I ended the call and sat back on my stool. *Cool, I'm invited to Billy Stone's office. How neat is that?*

Leaning over, the boom box's volume was turned back up. I returned to shining shoes for the rest of the evening.

CHAPTER THIRTY-THREE

I was on time for my appointment at Billy's office on Wednesday morning. As I entered the spacious lobby on the second floor, I saw gold records framed and hanging on the walls from one end to the other. Pictures of various country music singers, with Billy in the photos, also hung in clusters. There were a few concert posters positioned around the room, along with many other items. It was one impressive display showcasing what a star he'd become.

I walked up to the receptionist's desk, and before I could tell her my name, the lady seated there asked, "You must be the shoeshine guy?"

"Yes, that's me. This box I'm carrying must have given it away."

"No, I was expecting you at this time. Jackie, Billy's assistant, told me you were coming about now," she said. "Let me give her a call and let her know you've arrived."

Picking up her phone, the receptionist punched two numbers, waited a few seconds until Jackie answered, and said, "The shoeshine guy has arrived. He's smiling and ready to go. Sure. I'll send him to your office."

She hung up and directed me to go down a long hallway. "It's the second door on the right. Just walk on in when you get there. Jackie will be sitting out front and can direct you to Billy's office in the back."

"Thanks."

When I entered the room, Jackie was sitting at her desk looking over a few large photos spread out across the top.

She saw me and said, "Hello, Gary."

"Hello to you. You must be Jackie. We talked on the phone."

"Yes, we did. All Billy can talk about now is his personal shoeshine guy. You must have made a big impression on him. This morning, he brought in a bunch of cowboy boots and put them over in the corner. He's on the phone at the moment in his office, but you can go ahead and get started."

I placed my box on the floor next to the pile of boots, pulled out what I needed, and got down to business.

Jackie said, "So…you're going to start shining Billy's boots on a regular basis? Is that correct?"

"Yes ma'am. It sure looks like it."

"I know he's excited. He never seems to find the time to do it for himself…way too busy these days."

"I understand. For me to get to shine a country music legend's boots is a big deal. I don't mind it at all," I said.

"Billy will be here in a few minutes. His phone call won't

last much longer. He needs to look over these photos on my desk and choose the one he wants to use."

Just as Jackie finished with that statement, Billy walked out of his office. "There's my man," he said.

"Hey. How you doin'?"

Walking over to stand beside me, he shook my hand. "I told you there was plenty of work coming, didn't I?"

"Yes, you did. That is one large pile of fancy cowboy boots you own. I'll have them all lookin' good in no time."

"I've got to help Jackie pick out a photo. Go ahead and continue what you're doing. We can talk more in a little while."

Billy walked to her desk and began to gaze at the photos she had spread all over it.

He picked up one of them and set it aside. "I don't like that one at all." Pointing at two of the others, he said, "I really like both of these. Gary, come over here and give me your opinion about which of these photos you like the best."

As I got up and walked to her desk to stand beside Billy, Jackie said, "I like these two. They're the same ones Billy likes."

I asked, "What are they going to be used for?"

"They're for an advertising promotion...will be used on posters to be spread all around town before an upcoming country music concert," Billy answered.

"That makes the selection very important," I said. "In my opinion, I also like the two you've picked out, but the one on the left is my favorite."

"In that case," Billy said, "we'll use the one on the left.

I like it that you have a strong opinion, and your selection agrees with mine and Jackie's."

"Jackie, when will you send this one over to Tommy?"

"First thing tomorrow morning." She then looked down at the photos once again. "This one…yeah…I like it a lot."

"I believe it's the best one." Billy said, as he gathered the remainder of them into a single stack.

"OK. I'll get it over to Tommy. I've got to also call Merle about this weekend. Do you need to talk with him?"

"Naw, I don't think so," Billy replied.

CHAPTER THIRTY-FOUR

Jackie left the room to attend to other business, while Billy sat down in a chair close to me, and I continued to work.

"Are those boots in bad shape?"

"No...not at all. But, they're soon going to look better than they have in a long time."

"That's the attitude. I like the way you think."

Picking up one of the boots I'd just finished, he turned it around in his hands to check it out.

"I've never had them done like this. Wooo...doggy...lookin' good. So, what made you get into the shoeshine business?"

"To be honest with you, I had a bad car wreck a number of months ago. In the ambulance, on the way to the hospital, I didn't see a white light or anything, but I did hear a strange voice while I was semi-conscious. As it's turned out, the voice led me to a very special person. Now, don't think I'm crazy. He's the one that got me into doing this."

Billy paused for a moment and developed a slight smirk on his face.

I looked at him and asked the question, "Wasn't what you expected to hear, was it?"

Billy replied, "Well…not exactly. But, I'm glad you told me. I kind'a had the same type thing happen to me a couple of years ago. Did you hear about my wreck?"

"Yes, I did."

"Did you see the pictures they put in the paper from the accident? They were everywhere."

"Yes, I sure did."

"Pretty nasty, wasn't it? I shouldn't have survived that accident. Had been misbehaving badly that night, talking on my cell phone while driving. I admit I'd had a few too many before getting behind the wheel and ended up in intensive care for quite a while. I never told anyone, except my wife, but I think I also heard from someone like your special person shortly after the wreck. A few days after I got out of the hospital, when I was looking at my smashed-up SUV, I said out loud, 'You're one lucky guy.' Then, I heard a voice say, 'Luck had nothing to do with it.' I turned around, and no one was there. I knew I heard a voice…I just knew I did."

"I believe you," I said.

"Thank you. I'm glad you don't think I'm crazy."

"Did the voice say anything else?"

"Not just then, but shortly afterward, I encountered a man whose voice matched what I'd heard. He was very nice, but it sure was strange. In our conversation, he told me I'd been saved for a reason…that I wasn't finished and had more work to do. He said the work involved young people…that in time I'd figure it all out. I saw the man only that one time. Since then, I've been trying hard to find out what he meant."

Pausing for just a moment to think through what he wanted to say, he continued, "I've had a great career…got lots of good friends. I could stop now, but I know I've got some more left in me…I'm sure of it. I just don't know what I'm supposed to do next. It's really been bothering me. Do you understand what I mean?"

"Yes sir. I think I do. Billy…let me think this through with you. You've got a wonderful gift just waiting to be shared with others. And nobody can give it but you. You're the king of country music. You're kind'a like the top guy. You got there the hard way, for sure. It's been a long, rough road with lots of hard knocks…lots of scars." Pausing to consider what should be said next, I asked him, "They wanted you to be on that show *Country Star*, didn't they?"

"Yeah, they did."

"Here's a suggestion for you. There's a lot of young singers coming on the scene. You can help them like no one else can. Go on the show. Sing some of your old songs that a lot of those younger kids haven't heard. Let 'em hear what real country sounds like. Then, take ten of the finalists in the music contest, five guys and five girls, and make a CD with them. Bring back those old songs of yours with new blood. Name the CD, *Singing with the King*. Take those ten individuals on the road. You can really help those kids. Show 'em the ropes. Help guide them. Give them advice from the wealth of your experience. They'll be learning from the real country music King."

"Son, I think you may have something there."

Leaning back in his chair, he stopped and thought about what I'd just said.

I quickly said to Billy, "Actually, I don't know for sure where all of that came from. The concept just popped into my mind, and I blurted it out."

"Wherever it came from, that sounds like an excellent plan. In fact, it's genius." He got up and started walking all around the room. "*Singing with the King.* Heck, I can put out songs that I did forty years ago…songs older than the kids, for sure. Songs their mamas and daddies sang. Using some of my good ole country songs. We can make the old…new again."

"Exactly."

"You know, you'll have to go on the road with me…at least, some of the time. You gotta help me shine in more ways than one."

"I can do that," I said.

Billy rose from his chair and walked up to me. He patted me on the back and said, "I've gotta make some phone calls." Then he asked, "How much will I owe you when you finish all those boots?"

Before I could say anything, he decided for himself and reached for his wallet. He handed me two one-hundred dollar bills.

"Here. It's worth every penny of that to me, just to get those boots shined. I should be paying you much more for the idea. Your fantastic suggestion has just recharged an old man. Thanks. You're something else for a shoeshine guy. You know that? You've got a pretty good gift. And, I ain't talking about just shining shoes either."

He shook my hand. "It's a dang honor to know you, son."

"Thank you. You too, Billy."

Billy walked through the door and stood for a moment in the hall. He looked to the left before saying loudly, "Jackie, come to my office, please."

CHAPTER THIRTY-FIVE

Inside his office, Billy sat behind his desk in deep thought, staring out his window. Jackie had just pulled up a chair.

"Yes sir. What can I do for you?"

"Gary just gave me a tremendous idea. This could be big. I've been struggling with what I could do with my music and my life for a long time. I've needed a new direction. When I mentioned that to him, he came up with something I really like. I believe he's sparked in me a way to revive myself and my career, and it will end up benefiting many others, especially young people."

With that, Billy rose from his chair and started walking around the room. It was obvious he was excited.

He said, "Ok. Here it is. Listen to this. I go on the TV show *Country Star* and promote a special country music contest. With the ten finalists, of which five will be the top male and five will be the top female performers, I make a CD with them. I'll call it *Country Stars Singing with the King* and in the process I'll use some of my old songs. The contest will gain momentum and nationwide interest by letting the kids and everyone else know the top ten finalists will go on tour with me and perform shows across the country."

Jackie thought about what Billy had just said for only a short time before saying, "Wow! You're telling me the shoeshine guy came up with that?"

"Sure did. What do you think?"

"It's an amazing idea. I guess I need to call Bonnie Wilson and get started putting all of this together. I'm even getting excited thinking about it."

"Yep. Let's get on it quick, and let me know what I need to do to help."

Jackie got up from her chair and walked across the room with an obvious bounce in her step. Her enthusiasm about what she knew it could turn into had her mind going in all directions.

She turned, and just before leaving the office said, "You're right. This could be really big."

Billy sat back down at his desk for a couple of minutes, stared out the window, and finally said out loud, "*Singing with the King…*I like that."

About that time, Billy's phone rang, and he picked it up. It was Jackie again, but she was just letting him know there was a phone call for him on line one.

"You're going to be really surprised with this one. There's a lady from the White House wanting to talk with you."

"Thanks, Jackie. Get to work on the other stuff, and I'll

take the call." Billy picked up his phone and said, "This is Billy Stone."

"Mr. Stone. This is Martha Clayton at the White House. The President would like to speak with you. Can you take his call?"

"Certainly. I'd love to talk with him." Pausing a few seconds until he heard the President's first words of greeting, he said, "Hello to you, Mr. President. I'm doing just fine…how 'bout you? Sure…go ahead." After pausing to hear what the President had to say, he responded, "Next month? At your ranch? Sure, I can." Looking over at the calendar on his desk, Billy then said, "I don't have anything I can't cancel. Let's just plan for it. Fishing? You bet your boots. Color me in. I'll have my assistant, Jackie, call Martha to take care of the particulars. Good deal. I can't wait. See you then, partner. Bye."

Hanging up his phone, Billy lifted it again and pushed the button which went directly to Jackie's phone out front. "Jackie, can you come in here a minute?" Billy said, his mind surging with excitement about the call.

She quickly walked into the room.

"Yes sir."

"The President wants me to play at his birthday bash next month on the 18th…at his ranch. Actually, he wants me to be there a couple of days early, so he and I can do some fishing. You remember, Martha, his secretary? Call her and set everything up for me, please."

"I'll be glad to do it. You haven't seen the President in a while, have you?"

"No. But, it'll be great fun. Me and the President…fishing together. Can't wait."

Chapter Thirty-Six

Riding in Billy's travel bus, six of his musical friends sat around watching, as Billy and I played cards.

Billy said, "I'll raise you one dollar."

"OK. Show me what you've got," I replied.

"How 'bout a full house?" Billy said, as he laid his cards on the table.

"You're certainly a lucky guy. So, how much do I owe you, now?"

"Four dollars."

One of the guys sitting to the side said, "Whoa. You'd better watch it. He'll break ya."

From the front of the bus, a voice said, "Hey, guys. We're here."

Billy walked to the front, turned, and said to me, "Come here…check this out."

I walked to where Billy was standing, and we looked out the front window of the bus. In the distance was a big, white ranch house.

"Isn't that something?"

"Wow! Is that his other White House?"

"Yep. That's it."

A small group of secret service agents stopped the bus and entered with big smiles to welcome us.

Our bus driver said, "Whad'ya say, fellas?"

"How's it going, Gus? Hey, Billy."

"It's still going," Gus said.

"Still going? That's good," the agent replied.

Billy spoke up, "How're you doing? Haven't seen you in a while."

"Ahh. Same ole, same ole."

"Yeah, but sometimes that's good."

"You've got that right. It's always good to be here at the ranch. The Cowboy's in a much better mood at the ranch. He's over in his playroom right now. Been there all morning… stringing all the fishing rods, going through the tackle boxes… checking to make sure he has everything you two guys will need. He's getting ready to do some serious fishing with you, Billy."

"Good. I'm ready. I'll enjoy an afternoon of relaxation with the President."

Billy noticed one of the agents looking at me.

"Boys, this is my new shoeshine guy and companion, Gary Neal."

"Hello," the first agent said. "Glad to meet you."

Glancing over at Billy, he asked, "A shoeshine guy? Really?" He then looked down at his own shoes.

"Yep," Billy said.

"Hmmm…cool," the agent responded.

CHAPTER THIRTY-SEVEN

One of the agents showed the driver where to park the bus. Just to the side of the main building was a nice guest house, and we were invited to use it for our stay. The secret service agents got off the bus, and we followed.

We entered the guest house with our bags and suitcases. Everyone quickly chose a bedroom for themselves or one that had twin beds, so the room could be shared. A few of the men sat down to rest in the living room, and one turned on the TV to a sports show. Billy sat on the couch near the television, and I took a seat in a chair across from him.

An agent walked in and said, "If you need something to drink, soft drinks or bottled water, they are available, as many as you can drink, in the fridge."

I went over, got a bottled water, and brought one back for Billy. Just as I sat down again, the agent approached Billy.

He said, "Mr. Stone, the President would like you to

168 JIM HEARN AND ED HEARN

come over to the rec room. He wants to show you his new fishing rods."

Billy got up, turned around, and said to everyone, "Gentlemen, you'll have to excuse me. The President needs me."

He turned to the agent, "Let's go, son. Take me to your leader."

"You hang in there," he said to me. "Supper will be in a couple of hours. I was told they'll bring it in here. The President and I are gonna go play with his new toys."

He leaned over to me and whispered in my ear, "Hey, this is cool...ain't it?"

"Yes, it is. Very cool."

Billy left the room, and I turned the volume up on the TV with the remote.

CHAPTER THIRTY-EIGHT

As Billy entered the rec room with the agent, he saw the President looking through his tackle box.

"Hey there, Mr. President."

"Come on in here, you ole possum." He walked across the room to shake Billy's hand. "How you doing, ole buddy?" The President asked, as he placed his hand on Billy's shoulder.

"Finer than frog hair."

"Good to hear it."

"You're looking well in spite of having been under so much pressure running this here country."

With that, the President reached down and patted his stomach. "I've put on a few too many, but other than that, I'm feeling pretty good."

Billy picked up one of the fishing rods and said, "Wooo… weee…lookie here."

"Nice, huh?"

"Nice ain't the word for it."

Billy began to flip the rod as he walked around the room, acting as if he was in a boat and doing some serious casting.

"You're welcome to use that one, if you want to."

Billy just kept flipping it up and down, having a good time. "You know what, I think I will. Yep…this is the one for me," Billy said.

The President looked down at the boots Billy was wearing. "Are those the same boots I had made for you a couple of years ago?"

"Sure are. I wondered if you'd recognize 'em."

"I almost didn't. They look brand new. You must not wear them much. I know you didn't put that shine on them."

"Nope," Billy said. "I've got my own shoeshine guy now… brought him with me."

Billy then snapped his fingers, as a thought entered his head. "I just thought of something. How much time do you have?"

The President looked down at his watch and replied, "I've got to go over a couple of drafts of speeches in about half an hour…nothing 'til then. Why?"

"I want my guy to shine your boots. How does that sound?"

"Lord. I haven't had my boots shined in…I don't know how long. That sounds like a winner. I'll meet you in my office."

"OK. I'll go get him."

CHAPTER THIRTY-NINE

When Billy entered the guest house, I was sitting on the couch watching a ball game with the others.

He said, "Shine. Come with me. I've got some special boots I need you to do before supper. They're over in the next building."

I got up, and with my box, followed Billy.

We walked through two big doors on the side of the main building and entered a large open space with lots of comfortable seating. Two secret service agents had been standing at the doorway. One was a big, tall man named Earl. I knew that because of the name tag that was attached to his coat. I stood inside the large room for just a few seconds thinking about the man's name tag.

With a slightly puzzled feeling, I realized I'd seen Earl somewhere in the past. A vision suddenly entered my head of being at the diner in Nashville and having gone over to Jim's table, just as four men were leaving. One of those four was definitely Earl. I was sure of it. Earl must have sensed that I recognized him, because just moments earlier, he had winked at me as I passed.

Billy and I entered the President's office off to one side of the building.

"Shine. I want you to meet someone. This is your President."

Seeing the President caught me off guard. I just froze and stared.

"Mr. President, this is Gary Neal," Billy said.

The President extended his hand, and I slowly extended mine. We shook, as I struggled to gain my composure.

"Gary, nice to meet you."

I'm sure I had a surprised look on my face, as I glanced over at Billy and then back to the President. "Nice to meet you, Mr. President."

"Billy tells me you put a heck of a shine on a pair of boots." Pointing to Billy's boots, he asked, "Ya think you could do that…to these?" He then pointed down to his own cowboy boots.

I looked again at Billy, still in awe.

"Those are the special boots I wanted ya to do," Billy said with a smile. "Well…get busy. You ain't gettin' paid to stand around doing nothing."

The President sat down at his desk, and I followed him. I placed my shoeshine box to the side and pulled out all the necessary items. Down on one knee behind his desk, I got started on his boots. My mind shifted back to the statement Jim had made to me at the Y. *A man's gift makes room for him and brings him before great men.*

It was the same day Jim had also told me, **you never know whose shoes you might shine someday**. At the time, I had no idea that shining shoes could lead to this. I looked inside the box and noticed the picture of Abby. The thought entered my mind that she had not understood then what I felt I had to do. I continued shining the President's boots, one at a time.

I heard someone enter the room and walk to the front of the President's desk.

"Mr. President. Here's the draft of your speech for the teacher's convention," a lady's voice said.

After handing it to him, she just stood still, while he looked it over. Abby then noticed that someone was down on one knee shining the boots of the President behind his desk. She could only see the top of my hat and didn't see my face. She looked back up at the President.

The President said, "Let's see here."

Mumbling to himself, while reading the speech that Abby had written, his serious look changed to a smile.

He quoted, "We all have had a special teacher in our past… one that we have fond memories of. One that we respected… admired…and loved dearly. We all have known a teacher with that *special gift*. I know that **a man's gift makes room for him**…"

At that, I looked up and finished the line at the same time as the President read it. We both said together, "…**and brings him before great men**."

At that moment, Abby noticed me and her mouth flew open in total disbelief.

"Gary?"

I looked at her with a shocked expression on my own face.

"Abby?"

The President asked, "You two know each other?"

"We used to," I said, with a smile.

"That's right, Abby, you used to live in Nashville when you worked for the governor of Tennessee. How did you get to know Gary?" the President asked.

Looking directly at Abby, I answered before she had a chance, "We used to date."

"WHAT????" The President said, with a surprised expression. Smiling, he put his elbow on the edge of his desk and a finger to his temple. He then looked at Abby before adding, "Really?"

Trying to gain some composure, Abby cleared her throat and said, "Yes sir, that's the truth."

"My...My...MY. Isn't it a small world?"

I looked at Abby, who looked back at me. She lowered her eyes. I could tell she was trying not to tear up. I was sure she remembered our conversation when we were together at the restaurant on our final evening together.

I quickly thought about what had been said at that time. *There's something special in my future by shining shoes. When it happens, I want you there. I want you to be a part of it. I want to share it with you.*

Smiling, I told Abby, "You look great."

She smiled awkwardly and mouthed back, "Thank you."

The President had continued reading the speech and began to smile again. "This is unbelievable stuff! ***A man's gift makes room for him and brings him before great men***. Hmmmmm...I love it. That's a great line."

Looking at Abby, he asked her, "How did you come up with that one?"

"I heard someone quote it once," she said, while continuing to look directly at me. "That person is now shining your boots."

I spoke up and said, "It came from the Old Testament, sir. I believe it came from the Book of Proverbs."

The President said, "Really? That's great."

What ran through my mind was, *I can't believe she used that line in a speech for the President of the United States.*

The President said to me, "I've never heard it before, but obviously, you have. It must have made a big impression on you, if you memorized it."

"Well…I not only memorized it, I've seen it come true… many times."

"How so?" he asked.

"Take Billy, for instance. I was making my rounds to car dealerships one day and stopped at a Cadillac dealership, just south of Nashville. Billy was there working a deal on a car. The manager I've known for twenty years told me to follow him, because he wanted me to meet someone special. Next thing I knew, I was shining Billy Stone's boots."

Laughing and looking at Billy, he said, "How 'bout that?"

I continued, "Then, think about this…because of knowing Billy, I ended up right here…shining your boots. What are the odds of a traveling shoeshine guy from Nashville, Tennessee, shining the boots of the President of the United States? When I first started doing this, I didn't even think I could shine a car salesman's shoes…much less yours. Here in this moment, knowing where I've come from, I can't imagine it getting any better."

The President asked, "You've only been doing this for a fairly short time?"

"Yes sir. That's right."

"What made you get into this? What did you do before?"

"I was always in the car business. One day, I had a very bad car wreck…totaled the car. It was nasty…should have killed me. Actually, it may have."

"What do you mean?"

"On my way to the hospital in the ambulance, they say I was gone for over five minutes. No heartbeat, no blood pressure…not even breathing. Then, all of a sudden, everything was fine…back to normal. When I walked out of the hospital, though, I had a whole new outlook on life. From that day on, I saw things totally different. Especially, what I was doing and why. There was no explanation given for what had occurred. The doctor said he'd never experienced anything like it."

"What happened after that?" he asked.

"I met a…man. He told me about *a man's gift*. I wish you could meet him. I wish everybody could." After saying that, I paused and collected myself before continuing. "Anyway…he made me realize this road could take me to greatness. It has taken me to places and people I never imagined. I've found that by giving away my gift, I've received a lot more in return than money could have ever given me. Before this, only money motivated me. Now, I want to make a difference." Pausing again, for only a moment, I went on. "I don't know, maybe a part of me did die in the ambulance that day. I just know that I never dreamed I could be so happy doing something so simple. I realized that by touching the soles of my customers' shoes, I got to touch their souls on the inside. Sounds pretty corny, huh?"

"No sir…not at all," said the President.

I stopped shining his boots, looked up, and asked, "What do you think?"

Looking down at his boots, he exclaimed, "Have mercy! Billy, by golly, you were right. This is the best shoeshine I've ever had."

The President stood and began walking around the room, staring down at his boots. "Yes sir, these things are shining like a brand new penny. Even my man at the White House can't get this kind of shine."

He walked over to Abby and asked, "How in the world did you let this guy get away?" Walking back over to me, he asked, "How much do I owe you?"

"Nothing, sir. It was my pleasure."

"Hogwash."

The President pulled out his wallet and removed a fifty dollar bill. "How about this?"

"Whoa…I only charge eight dollars for boots."

"Son…you're worth more than you think."

I laughed and replied, "I've heard that before, also."

He extended his hand to me and said, "Thanks for a good conversation and a good shine…worth more than fifty dollars. It was a pleasure meeting you."

I shook his hand and said, "Sir, the pleasure was all mine… believe me." Handing him back the fifty-dollar bill, I asked, "Will you sign it for me?"

"Be glad to."

The President carefully signed his name and something else across the face of the bill and handed it back to me. I read it out loud.

"To Gary Neal, the best shoe…" I choked up a bit and then continued reading. "…shine guy I know." He had followed that statement with his signature in large script. Shaking his hand once more, I said, "Thank you, Mr. President. I appreciate it more than you'll ever know."

Then, I walked over to Abby who was standing close to the President.

I said, "It was good to see you, Abby."

Teary eyed, she replied, "It was good seeing you. I guess I don't have to ask what you've been doing since we were last together. You've been doing exactly what you said you'd be doing." Hesitating only briefly, she said, "I'm glad you found what you were looking for. It really looks good on you." She took my hand and finished by saying, "Take care."

"I'm glad things turned out well for you, too. You look fantastic. Take care of yourself."

After kissing her hand, just like in the past, and picking up my shoeshine box, I started to leave the room. Looking over at Abby, she looked down and then back up…tears in her eyes. She started to say something as a tear rolled down her face, but closed her eyes and said nothing. I stared at her with a blank expression. I had no words.

Billy, who had been quiet most of the time, looked at the President and said, "I'll be right back." To me, he said, "I'll walk out with you." Abby stayed in the room with the President.

We both left the room together but stopped outside the office in the hallway.

Billy said, "Hey...how about that?"

Still stunned, I replied without thinking. "Yeah...how about that? She's something, isn't she?"

"Not her...I meant shining the President's boots. Son, did you ever think you'd shine the boots of the President of the United States?"

"No sir, I didn't. But, I have a feeling someone else did."

"You know something...you were right," Billy said.

"About what?"

"**A man's gift does make room for him and brings him before great men**. There's more truth in that statement than we both know."

I left the room and walked back toward the guest house. On the way, I had a flashback of talking to Jim at the Y, when he had told me I didn't know whose shoes I might shine someday. I couldn't seem to get that statement out of my mind.

Laughing a bit and shaking my head, I said out loud, "Well Jim, you were right." After thinking more about what had just happened, I stopped and thought to myself, *Gary, you've just shined the President's boots.* I continued walking to the guest house to join the others.

CHAPTER FORTY

After both Abby and I left the room, the President sat at his desk and pushed a button on his phone to talk with Carol.

"Yes sir. Can I help you?"

"Is Jim in there with you?"

"Yes sir, he is."

"Send him in here, please."

Jim walked into the President's office and sat down in a chair in front of his desk.

"That program the First Lady is putting together, *Give Your Gift Away*, helping kids all across America find their talents and helping others reach their full potential. Have you had any luck finding the person to help her set up that program in the schools?"

"Still working on it, sir," Jim said.

"Remember when I made the comment, 'I hope we find the right person,' and you said, 'I have a feeling we'll recognize the person who is right for the job soon after meeting him or her?' Well, I think I found him."

"Really?"

"Yeah, and you won't believe what he does for a living."

"What's that?"

"He's a traveling shoeshine guy," the President said.

"Are you sure he's the best person for the job?"

"No doubt about it, and you won't believe where he's from."

"Where's that?" Jim asked.

"Nashville, Tennessee. I guess he's going to be another good thing that comes out of Nashville. I can't wait for you to meet him. He's really something else. You ought to hear his story. He was in the used car business for years, walked away from it, and started shining shoes. He was just in here and shined my boots. Billy Stone brought him here…" He hesitated just a little and then continued. "…from Nashville."

"How about that?"

"I'll get with the First Lady and have her assistant call him to set up a meeting. You can meet him then."

"Sounds great, sir. Looking forward to meeting him." Jim got up from his chair and started to leave the room but added one more thing. "I'm happy for you, sir."

"I'm happy about it, too." Shaking Jim's hand, he said, "Thank you."

Jim walked through the door and closed it on his way out. Passing Earl in the hallway, who was on guard there, he gave Earl a smile and then a wink, before continuing on his way.

CHAPTER FORTY-ONE

A week later, I was back in Nashville and in Dimples Diner for breakfast. While sitting at my favorite booth reading the newspaper, I looked up and was shocked to see Abby standing in front of me. She sat down across the table with a smile I'd have to call glowing.

"Hey. Good morning," she said.

"Hey! What brings you back to Nashville? Is the President in town?"

"No."

"Then, why are you here?"

"I came to visit an old friend."

"Who?"

"You."

"You came to Nashville just to see me?"

"Yes."

"Why?"

Waiting a moment, to make sure she said what was on her mind, she started, "When I saw you shining the President's boots, I couldn't believe it. It didn't seem like you at first. I mean, it wasn't the 'you' I used to know." She hesitated and then continued. "There you were doing exactly what you said you'd do someday. I never fully understood what you meant when you first told me that **a man's gift makes room for him and brings him before great men**. Not until…not until that very moment. Now I understand. That *crazy thing* you had to do, brought you to the feet of the most powerful man in the world."

"Yes, it did."

"And…I could see how happy you were. I could see how much you loved it. You weren't just shining his boots…you were giving him a part of you." She paused, looked down, and then back at me. "I didn't know you had it in you…giving that much love. I mean…I'll never forget what I saw."

My phone began to ring. I said, "Pardon me just a moment, so I can answer this. Don't go anywhere. I'm excited about seeing you."

"This is Gary…Yes, ma'am. I'm the shoeshine guy." I paused for only a second when I was told it was the First Lady's assistant. "The White House?" Looking at Abby with a startled expression on my face, I continued to listen. "Can I hold for the First Lady? Yes, ma'am." Mouthing to Abby in a low whisper, "the White House has me on hold for the First Lady."

Abby looked surprised. She said, "The First Lady? What is she doing calling you?"

Back on the phone, I was listening as the First Lady started to talk. I said very quickly, "Hello, Mrs. Presid.....Madame First Lady."

Abby's mouth dropped open, as she listened to my end of the conversation.

"Yes, ma'am. I have plenty of time to talk. Yes, I'll try to."

Looking across the table directly at Abby, I tried to contain my excitement as the First Lady told me the good news.

"You want me to help you with a new program? No, ma'am, I haven't got anything important going on here." After a moment, I responded again to what she was saying. "Hmmm...*Give Your Gift Away*...to benefit younger people...that sounds pretty cool."

I was looking at Abby across the table and listening to the First Lady explain as my eyes opened wider. I couldn't believe what I was hearing.

"Can I come to the White House to talk about it?"

With that, Abby gave me an even more shocked look.

"I would be glad to. Yes...you can call me anytime. Yes, ma'am. I'm looking forward to our visit, too. Oh...you're welcome. Goodbye."

I ended the call and looked at Abby in total disbelief. Swallowing hard, I said, "I'm going to the White House to meet with the First Lady."

"What for?"

"She wants me to help her with a new program she's starting in schools across America called *Give Your Gift Away*. She said she wanted to sit down with me and have me help her set up the program. Then, tour with her when she goes to different schools all across the country and maybe give some speeches. It would require me to move to Washington to work with her and help her oversee what she's doing."

Abby said, "I knew she was working on a new program… something really important. I just didn't know the details."

Pausing and then realizing what had just taken place, Abby began to speak slowly.

"If she goes to schools and gives speeches, I'll have to write them for her." Pointing to me, she continued. "And, if you give speeches…I'll have to work on them with you."

I was absolutely stunned with what Abby had just said, but she continued.

"If you're going to work with her, that means you and I will be working together…WOW!"

Looking serious and directly into Abby's face, I leaned forward and asked, "Is this a dream?"

"Yes, it's actually your dream come true."

She began to tear up and asked me, "Remember our last night together at the restaurant in Nashville?"

"How could I forget? Yes."

"You said there was something big out there waiting for you. And, you had to go find out what it was. When you found it, you wanted me to be there."

With that, she began to sob and looked up at the ceiling while tears rolled down her cheeks. She took a deep breath and exhaled.

"You wanted me to share it with you." Looking directly at me, she said, "It looks like you've got your wish."

I leaned back in my seat and said, "WHOA!" Glancing

slightly to the side and then back at her face, I moved forward. "Are you OK with that?"

Abby looked at me with a piercing and loving look. Then, speaking confidently, she said, "Absolutely. Actually, I'm more than OK with it."

"What do you mean?"

"My purpose in coming here in the first place was to ask you a question, but it just got answered."

"What was the question?"

"I wanted to ask you if there was any chance we could get back together. I realized last week at the ranch what you meant about *a man's gift bringing him before great men*. It made me wonder if it could do the same for me. Now, I know it will. My gift and your gift…working together. We will be experiencing your dream together." She took my hand and asked, "Are you OK with that?"

"Absolutely…I'm more than OK."

Abby then asked, "I'm going to need some help. Will you help me?"

"You can count on it," I answered. "I'll be there for you."

Just as that was said, our waitress came over and asked Abby, "Coffee for you, Sweetie?"

"Please."

She poured Abby a cup and then asked me, "How 'bout you, Honey?"

"Yes, please."

She poured a cup for me.

As the waitress started to walk away, I asked her, "Where's April?"

"She called in sick today."

"Are you new?"

"I'm new here."

"What's your name?"

"Ann."

"Ann?"

"Just Ann."

With that, she gave me a look and an unusual smile. I stared at her name tag and saw it only contained her first name. There was no last name...like the others. She saw me looking and winked. Then, she walked away.

A big smile formed on my face. I took a sip of my coffee and looked across the table at Abby.

I said to her, "Abby, I think help is on the way."

On the radio, playing softly in the background, I heard a nice song begin. It was a romantic one named *At Last.*

Leaning over, I asked Abby, "May I have this dance?"

She smiled and took my hand. Rising, we both embraced and began to slow dance beside the table in the diner. She laid her head on my shoulder, and I knew everything was going to be just fine.

A Special Tribute to Gary Neal Armstrong

By Jim Hearn

Gary Neal Armstrong, in real life, was a special person and a good friend of mine. I originally met him at a local YMCA while working out in 2003. He was from Madisonville, Kentucky but lived near me in Brentwood, Tennessee. When we met, he was shining shoes at the Y in the mornings, going to shine car salesmen's shoes at various dealerships during the day, and then back to the Y in the afternoon. While working, he always wore nice clothes and could usually be seen with a stylish hat or cap. All of that was part of his desire to present himself as a person with true class.

At first, I was amazed a guy as talented as Gary was shining shoes for a living. After I got to know him better, he shared with me many of his struggles and accomplishments that led to that occupation. With a BS degree from Belmont University in Nashville, Gary had taught school for a short time and later enjoyed a very successful sales career in the used car business.

He loved music and swing dancing in particular. Even though he had gone through a very bad divorce, his marriage produced a daughter, whom he loved more than anything.

His biggest life struggle was that he suffered from diabetes, which had taken his two older brothers. Gary constantly monitored his condition and tried to take care of himself. Stress from various jobs and not eating properly caused his problem to get out of control, so on the advice of a doctor, he quit all his lucrative jobs and began to simply shine shoes for a living.

I found Gary to be one of the funniest and most sensitive individuals I ever knew. Usually, I couldn't be near him without either laughing or crying because of something he did or said. One of his side jobs was working for a new car dealer on weekends, where he dressed as a clown and hawked customers from the street and into the dealership.

He sold old shoes that were purchased from Goodwill, which he had re-conditioned to look like new. I recall several trips, when I accompanied Gary to the local Goodwill outlet store, while he shopped for shoes. It was like going to the county fair with a child because we had so much fun.

I really don't know exactly what bonded us, but after a year or two of being friends, Gary started calling me his guardian angel. I was embarrassed the first time he called me that, but he was just showing me his appreciation for some things I regularly did to assist him. I was known at the Y for always wearing an NFL football jersey with the number 89 on the back, which was the number of my favorite football player. Those two things were later tied together in our story.

Over a period of time, he was hospitalized several times with heart attacks caused by his diabetes. I was the only person he had to list as next of kin with the hospital. I visited him each time he was in the hospital and took him back to his motel room on release. Yes...a motel room. That was where Gary lived. He paid weekly and was always current on his rent. Everything he had in the world was stored in a small space in his motel room or in his truck.

Gary came to my home on many evenings. Sometimes he was hungry and didn't have money for food. One evening while visiting me at my home, and literally eating almost everything in my refrigerator, he told me he was scared he wouldn't live very long, as both his brothers had died at about his current age from diabetes.

He knew there were government programs that could be of assistance to him, but he refused to take any type of government help, as he viewed it as "welfare." He was too proud to accept any "handouts" and was convinced he could make it on his own. Many days it was a struggle for him to get to work, but he forced himself to face each day with a smile and an appreciation for what health he still enjoyed.

He told me about a bucket list of things he wanted to do and among them was to go to a Tennessee Titans' football game and also write a screenplay. I was able to invite him to an NFL game several months later, with the request that he wear his clown costume. He thought I was kidding, but I was never more serious, as I always dressed up for the games in a funny outfit. Gary did, in fact, wear his clown costume to the game, and we sat on the front row next to one another. That day, we were photographed by several national news organizations and the local newspaper. Later in the evening, he and I were highlighted on the national TV sports show, *Sports Center*, and Gary was blown away with the attention he received. The next day, photos of the two of us attending the game in our outfits appeared in the local newspaper. From then on, we were inseparable. We went to several more NFL games, and together wrote a full-length screenplay of *The Shoeshine Guy* during 2006 and 2007, completing Gary's two main bucket list items.

Gary occasionally depended on me for small monetary assistance, but at the same time he also worked very hard at shining shoes to earn money, regardless of how he felt because of his health condition. He and I began a routine of going to a local restaurant every night after working out so I could buy him a healthy meal for the day. He would take the lemon from my tea and put it in a glass of water to make himself lemonade in order to save me money for his drink.

A funny thing to me, which happened during that time, had to do with Gary's old pickup truck that seemed to be on its last mile. The door lock on the driver's side was broken, and he had to go around to the passenger side to lock and unlock the truck. He did that every time he parked because he carried almost half of his personal belongings in the truck. While visiting me once, I asked him why he didn't just take the good lock and swap it for the bad lock on the truck. He'd never thought about doing that. As a result, we spent most of the day swapping the locks and that made me a genius in his mind. It did save him a lot of time, and we laughed about it often.

One day in August of 2011, I received the sad news Gary had passed away in his motel room from another heart attack. Humble by nature and strong in spirit, Gary Neal Armstrong was an inspiration to me. I wish you had known him. If you had, he would have brightened your day and opened your eyes to many wonderful things in life.

The Shoeshine Guy, adapted from the original screenplay, tells of a very proud man who dropped everything to shine shoes for a specific reason. In Gary's case, one of the reasons he shined shoes was to encounter less daily stress in an effort to extend his life. Another of his reasons was the fact that he truly loved his customers. He firmly believed that by his personal interaction with them, and by sharing his special gift, he could make a difference in their lives.

A lot of the happenings included in this book are more truth than fiction. It will be up to you, the reader, to determine exactly what falls in each category, while you enjoy the story that closely parallels Gary's actual life.

In Remembrance

Included in the following random statements are a sampling of thoughts and impressions by friends and acquaintances of Gary that were found on the Internet in the latter part of 2011, shortly after his death. They show how much people respected and cared about him and his life. He was a positive influence on more people than he ever knew.

"Anyone who walked down the steps at the Y where Gary worked, between 2003 and 2011, no doubt saw Gary Neal Armstrong. The shoeshine guy held court in that spot for close to a decade."

"Starting in 2003, his post at the base of the steps grew from buffing a few pairs of shoes a day, to a rock-and-roll boom box empire of shoes stacked halfway up the wall waiting to be shined. He had occasional items for sale and the biggest assortment of Dum Dum lollipops in town."

"Walking up to Gary's usual spot this past Friday afternoon out of habit, near the bottom of the main staircase at the Y, I had a pair of shoes for him to shine. He was not there. Since 2003, Gary had worked at the same spot, and over the years I gave him a lot of business. It will be strange going down the stairs now and not hearing his soundtracks of 60s, 70s and 80s tunes playing from his old-school stereo he setup each time he was there. Even though I saw him almost every day, there's so much about him I never knew."

"It amazes me how we see people every day…talk to them…work with them…care about them, and still there is so much we don't know about them. Whether you miss his music, his trivia questions or his booming laugh, there will always be an empty place at the bottom of the stairs where we will remember."

"I knew Gary for a long time. Every day I would walk down the steps and say 'hi'. He was the sweetest man in the whole world. I miss him so much now. He will never leave my heart."

"We miss Gary for all he meant to our Y family. His area will never be the same. We miss his music, laugh, trivia and stories."

"Gary was known for his boom box blasting out almost every old song. It always helped me get my butt up the steps after a workout. Whatever song he was playing at the time, it usually made me smile and caused me to recall some crazy memory from my past."

"The first time I met Gary was at a Titans' football game when he was dressed up like a clown. That clown outfit got him on the Jumbotron, and he even made ESPN's sports highlights. He got the biggest kick out of that. He was a great man, had an amazing sense of humor, and touched many lives. Gary will be missed by many. I don't think he ever truly realized how many people loved and admired him. He often said that women wouldn't date him because of his job, and I would tell him that those women weren't worth dating. He had a lot of pride and honor. I respected him for never taking the easy road. Some encouraged him to go the welfare route because of his medical condition, but he would never consider that for a minute. He loved what he did, and he especially loved the people he met and spoke to each day while shining shoes. He may be gone but will never be forgotten."

About the Authors

Jim Hearn

A successful Nashville businessman, Jim lives in Brentwood, just south of the city. He owns and operates a variety of large companies in the area and possesses almost endless energy. Each day involves him tackling new projects for the benefit of himself and others.

The Shoeshine Guy is Jim's first attempt at writing a novel. With it, he worked with his brother Ed to create a valuable book to be shared with the world. Unique insights woven into the story are all part of his personal philosophy he uses each day. After reading the story, Jim hopes you will adopt those special concepts for your own.

Ed Hearn

A long-time resident of Nashville and now living in Wilmington, North Carolina, Ed has been writing non-fiction memoirs for a number of years. Currently, he has five of those books in print that are available on his webpage at https://www.amazon.com/Ed-Hearn/e/B07MLTZFHX

Ed teamed up with his brother to help write *The Shoeshine Guy*, which offers an intriguing and unusual tale. Their challenge was to present it in a creative way to engage the reader with a simple, but deeply meaningful story. With this new book, they hope that goal was achieved.

.

THE BOOKS OF WISDOM/WORKS

Wisdom/Works is a new cooperative, cutting edge imprint and resource for publishing books by practical philosophers and innovative thinkers who can have a positive cultural impact in our time. We turn the procedures of traditional publishing upside down and put more power, a vastly higher speed of delivery, and greater rewards into the hands of our authors.

The imprint was launched with the Morris Institute for Human Values, founded by Tom Morris (Ph.D. Yale), a former professor of philosophy at Notre Dame and a public philosopher who has given over a thousand talks on the wisdom of the ages. Wisdom/Works was established to serve both his audiences and the broader culture. From the imprint's first projects, it began to attract the attention of other like-minded authors.

Wisdom/Works occupies a distinctive territory outside most traditional publishing domains. Its main concern is high quality expedited production and release, with affordability for buyers. We seek to serve a broad audience of intelligent readers with the best of ancient and modern wisdom. Subjects will touch on such issues as success, ethics, happiness, meaning, work, and how best to live a good life.

As an imprint, we have created a process for working with a few high quality projects a year compatible with our position in the market, and making available to our authors a well-guided and streamlined process for launching their books into the world. For more information, email Tom Morris, Editor-in-Chief, through his reliable address of: TomVMorris@aol.com. You can also learn more at the editor's website, www.TomVMorris.com.

Made in the USA
Lexington, KY
23 November 2019

57579562R00129